# DARK LONGING

DARK SERIES
BOOK TWO

CASSIE HARGROVE

# TW/CONTENT

Dark Longing isn't nearly as graphic and dark as Book 1, but there are some notable differences, so please be mindful of the possible triggers listed below!

- mention of past SA
- BDSM and D/s dynamics
- drugging (for protection)
- some graphic mentions of violence

# 1

## DEVLIN

It's a madhouse in here.

Everyone and their goddamn father is here tonight, and I'm a girl short. Fuck my life with a cactus.

"Boss, we have a girl here looking for a job," my head of security says, stepping before me.

I know we're a girl down, and in reality, it's my fault, but the girls don't complain because they know I keep them safe. It's not that we lack applicants, I'm just extremely strict when it comes to who I will hire. We're an upscale club, and I have a lot of rules and guidelines that need to be met in order to hire someone, and most of the women interested in stripping simply don't make the cut.

I'm not a bastard. Fine, I am, but I don't have a

choice in situations like these. You can be hot as sin, and I'll still turn you down if you don't meet the requirements laid out in the application.

"We're a little busy tonight, Paul," I state, moving toward my office. I have calls to make and some paperwork to file.

No one ever tells you the true logistics of owning a strip club, and Jesus, it's a pain in the ass sometimes.

"Boss, you're going to want to take the time. Trust me," he says with a shit-eating grin on his face that gives me pause.

"Name?" After being with me for years, he knows how I work. He knows I expect him to grab this information before coming to me.

"Shelby Engels."

I scoff. "This isn't Little House on the fucking Prairie, Paul. Send her away. You know I don't have time to deal with little, innocent doves trying to get out from under Daddy's thumb by taking their clothes off." I shake my head in annoyance.

"Awfully fucking judgemental of you, don't you think?" a snarky voice says from behind him, making Paul chuckle.

I cut him a hard glare, effectively shutting him up and making him look like a scolded child.

"I didn't mean anything by it, but I don't have time right now. Paul here knows better than to bring anyone back here without my express permission." I don't know why I'm trying to explain myself to this woman.

"Engels happens to be a German name, you fucking nitwit," she snarls before stepping out from behind Paul.

I stop breathing the second I lay eyes on her.

She's tall and slender with long, blonde hair that frames her face and brings her bright blue eyes into focus.

When I can't form a goddamn sentence, she smirks like she's won something, and fucking hell, I think she has. She's won my undying loyalty to stalk her ass for the rest of my life. Or until I get bored like I always do.

But she's different. She's everything they weren't, I can tell, and I don't know how to process that realization.

I clear my throat and fix my suit vest, reminding myself I have a business to run. I definitely don't have time for some blonde-haired beauty to render me speechless.

Fuck, my best friend, Jonathan, is going to have a field day over this.

"You want to work for me?" I question, faking the cocky attitude I usually carry with ease.

"This is the only place that doesn't make me want to vomit just by walking through the door," she says with a shrug.

Wow, this woman has a lot of balls. She's not wrong about my place being the best, but the shit she's spewing doesn't make it sound like she actually wants to work here or anywhere like my club.

"If you're that opposed to strip joints, why are you here? You're taking up my time when I'm a girl short and needed elsewhere," I snap, not even caring that I've just insulted the woman I'm newly obsessed with.

I make a mental note to search for her details later as my phone vibrates. When I check it, I breathe a sigh of relief before turning and walking away. "Get rid of her, Paul. Beth needs me at the bar," I order, not turning back.

"Hey, asshole! It's clear you need help, so why are you fucking ignoring me?" little miss prairie hisses behind me.

I stop in my tracks, loving the fact she runs right into me before I turn around and move toward her until she's backed against the wall.

"I'm not looking to hire someone who turns her

nose down at what we do here," I tell her, loving the fire in her eyes. "My girls need these jobs to support their families. I don't have time for a little girl coming in here to apply for a job on a whim when she won't even last a month. You'll be taking tips from them just because you're new blood, and they deserve better than that." I shake my head, stepping away from her.

"I want this job, and I guarantee I won't quit after a month." She huffs and straightens her shoulders. "I'm not here to fuck with you."

I quirk an eyebrow, deciding I have a moment to hear her out. Shit, I'm a saint today... or obsessed with her. Probably the latter.

"Why do you want this job?" It's a simple question and one I ask every person I interview.

She narrows her eyes at me. "Look, I work for my best friend at a tiny dog grooming place. It's great to work for her and all, but I need something else. I need to feel free, you know?"

I can tell she's only being partially honest with me,. As much as I'd like to call her out on it, I get the feeling this is as close to the truth as I'm going to get from her. Her guards are too high. For her to give me the truth, she needs to be vulnerable.

Oh, I'll get the answers I seek. I'll learn everything there is to know about my prairie girl very soon. But for now, I have a business to run.

"If you fill out the paperwork, go through all of the checks like everyone else and pass? Maybe we'll talk." She lets out an adorable little growl, probably thinking I'm playing her. "Take it or leave it, prairie, but that's the deal. I don't change the hiring process for anyone. You will be treated as any other applicant."

I wait for her response for just a second. It's long enough to see a flicker of gratitude before it's flushed out by her snarkiness.

"Fine, boss man, you have a deal. But trust me…" She moves toward me and wraps her hand around my tie. "You won't think twice about hiring me once you see me up there."

She lets go of my tie before patting it down and walking around me, disappearing out of sight as I stand there like an idiot.

My dick is harder than it's ever been, and she didn't have to do anything other than be a pain in my ass. Fuck, I need to get it together, and I know just how to do it.

ME:

You busy?

JON:

Just playing. Why?

Fuck, he's insane. But I need his insanity right now. It's exactly the distraction I need to forget about Shelby fucking Engels until I have some more information to go on.

ME:

I need a distraction.

JON:

Another sightseeing adventure fall flat?

God, he's a smartass.

ME:

You know how easily I get bored.

JON:

Make it quick. Cat's already got his tongue. You're going to miss all the fun.

Sick bastard. I don't think I'm ready to find out what he means when he says that. The code we've established is far too vague, and that could undoubtedly mean anything. Though, if I had to guess...

> Right. See you in an hour. Make sure you have some cold beer. If I have to deal with your damn cats, I deserve some alcohol.

I pocket my phone and run my fingers through my hair to shake myself out of this obsessive pull Shelby seems to have brought out in me.

I've felt this pull a million times before, and I'll get through it the same way I always do. Even if it is stronger than usual this time.

I'll stalk her for a while, maybe fuck her out of my system, and move the fuck on.

And I will *not* hire her.

# 2

# SHELBY

THAT COCKY ASSHOLE. Where does he get the right to judge me like he fucking knows me even though we've never met?

Little House on the fucking Prairie, my ass.

God, that man irritates me, and I barely know him. So why am I still insisting on getting this job? It's not like I need it. Working for my best friend, Olivia, pays the bills just fine, but my nights are spent seeking a thrill through random hookups. And after sleeping with my ex from high school again, I'm over it.

I need to feel desired and wanted while also feeling an adrenaline rush. Sleeping with random men—when most of them can't even get me off—is just too goddamn depressing anymore.

Actually, I don't know why I hadn't thought of this sooner. I grew up dancing, and I'm good. Like really good. So, pole dancing should have been a logical choice, but it hadn't crossed my mind until a few days ago.

After hooking up with my ex the other night, I went for a drive to clear my head. That's when I saw this place. It's just outside of town on the way to the city, but it's in a neighbourhood I tend to avoid, given how rich it is. People like Olivia's brother and father live here, and I hate those assholes.

Getting back in the car, I dial Liv to check in with her, but it goes straight to voicemail which isn't like her.

Shit, I shouldn't have left her this afternoon after that fucker called her a fat cow. God, I hate men. He flat out ran into her when we stepped out of the shop because he wasn't looking where he was going, but rather than apologizing, he blamed her size on "taking up too much of the sidewalk".

I've never wanted to cut a bitch more than I did in that moment, and I'm still so fucking angry over it.

I hang up and try again, my skin starting to itch when she still doesn't pick up.

"I'm coming, Liv. Hold on," I whisper and put the

car in drive, heading back into town and toward her house, when my phone pings.

LIV:

> Please, don't worry about me. I just need some time. I'll call you later, okay?

Fuck, I hate when she insists on being alone like this when I know she's upset. I hated letting her walk away earlier, knowing she was headed home to cry, and I couldn't do anything about it.

Pulling over, I type out a quick answer to her.

ME:

> I'll hold you to that, babe.

\* \* \*

By the time I get home and settled, it's almost midnight, and I'm fucking tired. After Liv's text, I drove around for a while to distract myself until Liv sent me a text to say she was going to call.

As soon as my phone rings, I answer it, needing to hear her voice and know she's okay.

"Liv!"

She sighs down the line. "I'm okay, Shelbs. Just tired."

Just tired? Fucking lie, but I'll let it slide.

"Liv, I'm worried about you. Maybe you should try and get out more." I wince, knowing she's going to get pissed at me.

"What do you mean get out more?" she questions, her voice sounding suspicious.

"You know, just go to events. Maybe try to make some more friends. I feel like you avoid the world because of your family, and that's no way to live, babe." I wait for her to say something, but her silence is telling enough.

When she continues to not speak, I keep going, knowing this is going to make her lose it. "Maybe you should join a dating app."

"No. Absolutely not. Have you lost your mind?!" she shrieks, making me wince. "How did you go from my being insulted and called a fat cow to setting up a dating profile for me in the span of a few hours?"

Well, when she puts it like that. Shit. But I'll stick to my guns. I'm just trying to look out for her.

"I just think it would be a great way to meet other people," I explain.

"I'm not interested in dating anyone!" She's annoyed now. But hey, that's better than sad. I'll take her annoyance and anger over sadness any day.

"You can't be a virgin forever, Liv," I tell her, knowing she hates this conversation. I think she's truly afraid that no one will want her because of all the shit her father and brother have said to her over the years.

"I can too," she snarks, making me snort. God, I love this girl. She's so adorable and innocent.

"Fine," I huff, acting like I'm annoyed. "Let me rephrase that. Why the fuck would you want to remain a virgin forever? You need to go on dates, Liv."

It's a genuine curiosity of mine. Even shitty sex is still worth having, and eventually, she'll have someone rock her damn world. Then she'll realize why there are so many people willing to stalk and kill for sex.

Fuck, I need some of that hot-as-sin sex back in my life.

"I don't want to go on dates. The last thing I want is to meet someone like my father or brother, Shelbs," she hisses.

I fucking knew this was why she's so afraid to date, but it's the first time she's admitted it aloud. God, I hate those bastards. I wish they'd just disappear.

"Not all men are money-hungry, disgusting

assholes. Stop making the entire male population out to be bad guys," I tell her, gentling my tone a little.

Just because I have a general hatred for most men doesn't mean they're all bad. I'm just jaded as fuck, and I can be aware of that fact.

Olivia snorts down the line. "Right, because you've had great success in finding someone decent."

I sigh. She's not wrong, but still. "My sex life is mine, and mine alone. I don't want to date, but you're not the fuck em' and leave em' type." And she's not. I'm not sure I really am either, but men are a good distraction from taking life too seriously.

"It's late, Shelbs. We have to work tomorrow." Liv yawns into the phone, and I decide she needs to take a goddamn day off. She deserves it. She's always working way too hard.

"Actually, you don't. I've got it covered. If you even think about showing your face at the shop tomorrow, I'm going to spank you."

"You can't kick me out of my own shop!" she screeches, making me smile.

"I can. I did, and you won't stop me. You've been crying all night. Don't even try lying to me because I can hear it in your voice."

She's silent for a moment. "Fine. Thank you,

babe. I owe you," she says gently, and I let out a silent sigh of relief. I was worried she'd fight me harder on this.

"You totally owe me. Make me some of my favourite muffins, and we'll call it even." I joke, but she laughs and agrees before letting me go.

I hope she goes to sleep and spends tomorrow resting. She needs it.

Speaking of rest, if I'm opening the shop alone tomorrow, I need to get some damn sleep, too.

# 3

# DEVLIN

BY THE TIME I get down into Jonathan's hidden kill bunker, I'm more than ready to toss back a few beers and crash in his spare room.

Fuck this night, and damn my prairie girl for getting so deeply under my skin so easily.

"Wake up, you piece of shit. I'm not done playing with you yet," Jonathan taunts as I walk into the room and freeze at the sight in front of me.

"What in the actual fuck am I looking at? Jesus, I need something stronger than beer for this shit," I groan, my stomach rolling as I speak.

The guy is tied to a chair and barely alive. The lower half of his face is covered in blood that's dripped down to drench his shirt. It looks like his legs are also broken, both of them bent in unnatural directions, making my legs ache in commiseration.

Maybe the most disturbing thing, though, is seeing his hands mangled. His fingers have all been de-fleshed, and all that remains are the bones. It's disgusting.

"Thank fuck, you're here. I'm getting bored. Matthew here has no sense of humour." Jonathan shakes his head, looking at me. "They never laugh at my jokes."

I wince. "First off, I don't even know how to process everything in front of me. What the fuck did this guy do to you?"

A dark look crosses his face, one I haven't seen a whole lot of on my best friend. I know this side of him exists, but I've never really seen him get so... angry before.

"He's a snivelling little shit who should learn to keep his mouth shut. He pissed me off, and that's all I'm going to say," Jonathan states, his face shutting down.

There is clearly a lot more to it, but there's no way he's going to tell me about it. It's not like I'm in the best position to judge right now. I'm not exactly ready to tell him how this girl has flipped my head on its axis, either.

"Right," I state, and the guy groans.

I look over at him, and his bloodshot, exhausted eyes plead with me like I'm going to save him.

"Don't look at me like that. I'm not here to save you. You're the one that's stupid enough to piss off a serial killer, and I'm not about to do the same." I shake my head at him while Jon cackles. "Besides, you don't have a tongue or fingers anymore, and your legs are beyond fucked. Do you really even want to live the rest of your life like this?"

I watch him close his eyes and instantly know his answer. He doesn't. He'd give anything to just die now to be out of this situation, this pain.

"As for the other part of your comment..." I turn to Jon. "Maybe they'd be more receptive to your sense of humour if you weren't torturing them to death while you used it," I tell him, and he looks thoughtful for a second before smirking.

"I'd rather just torture them."

Yeah, not surprised.

"Scotch. I need the good shit, and I know you keep it down here somewhere," I tell him, giving him a look and daring him to argue.

"It's on my desk in the office. Had a drink earlier when this dumbass passed out."

Once I've got the bottle of scotch and come back

to the room, Jonathan slaps this guy in the face to try and wake him up. But I think he's a lost cause. I'm not even sure he's breathing anymore.

"It's so hard to find someone that can handle a good torture session," my best friend grumbles. "He's barely alive. Guess it's time for me to finish it and put the little shit out of his misery."

I shake my head, gulping down a good amount of scotch as Jonathan grabs a battery.

I am not drunk enough for this.

I drink some more while staring up at the ceiling, listening to the guy's screams as Jonathan pours acid onto him until the room is quiet. It's one of his favourite ways to finish the job before disposing of their bodies in larger vats of the shit.

"I need air," I state, the smell of burning flesh making me sick.

"I'll come with you. I'll deal with him when you leave," he says, coming up behind me.

I wait for him to wash his hands before we make our way up the stairs, through the hidden door in his garage floor, then outside.

"You're not yourself tonight," I state, watching him under the moonlight.

He shrugs. "Had some anger I needed to work out, but I'm good now." He turns to look at me. "He deserved everything he got and more," he states, taking the bottle I hold out to him before tossing his head back and drinking his fill.

"I trust you." I do. I believe him when he says that guy down there deserved whatever he got.

Jon may be a killer, but he doesn't harm the innocent. Never has and never will. He's a killer with morals, if you can believe that. And it takes a lot to truly piss him off like this.

"What brought you over here tonight, knowing I was playing? Usually, you avoid being around for that shit."

He's watching me closely like I was him, and I don't lie to him—I'd never lie to him—so I tell him the bare minimum of the truth.

"Let's just say work was beyond fucked tonight. I'm a girl down, and Beth almost shot some asshole at the bar for trying to grope one of the girls." I blow out a breath, and he laughs, handing the bottle back to me.

"You need this more than I do." He chuckles. "You know the spare room is always open. Go crash before that scotch hits you. I have to clean Matthew up and make him disappear."

"You good?" I check in with him one more time, and he runs his hands down his face.

He's covered in blood and other shit I don't even want to think about, and he looks really fucking tired. I've never seen him like this.

"I'm good. Just been a long few days. Sometimes living a double life can get tiresome, I guess," he says. "Go. You're going to fall on your face any minute, man." He laughs, shaking his head and turning to go back into the garage.

I nod and thank him before leaving him to do his thing and heading into the house.

He's not wrong. I can already feel the scotch in my system. I need to find a bed and crash.

# 4

# SHELBY

A DANCE.

One final test to see if I can cut it working for Devlin Thomas, and I know I have this in the bag.

I get the feeling he doesn't want me to succeed. He doesn't want to hire me—that much is easy to see —but he's down a girl, and he has no reason to turn me away.

I won't give him the option to say no to me. I a cheerleader and choreographed all of our routines in high school for a reason.

While some girls are chosen as head cheerleader because of their popularity and social standing, I was chosen for my dancing and skill set.

I was only popular in school *because* I was the head cheerleader, not the other way around.

If the great boss man expects to see me fail, he'll be waiting a damn long time.

"We don't have all day!" he shouts from the other side of the curtain, making me smirk.

I think I'm going to like making his life a living hell. It's only fair since he seems annoyed by my very presence. A girl's gotta have a little fun somehow.

I nod to the DJ, and *Pour Some Sugar on Me* by Def Leppard starts playing throughout the stage and sitting areas. It's cliché to use this song, but it's a feel-good tune for me.

Taking a deep breath, I waltz through the curtain and onto the stage, trying to not let the lights shock me. It's been a long time since I've been front and centre like this, and I momentarily forgot how blinding it can be.

As I adjust, I continue the routine I've practiced over a dozen times in the last couple of days and let the music guide me.

I roll my hips to the beat, moving and shaking what God gave me as I reach the pole.

*Breathe, Shelby. This is just like the classes you take in the city. It doesn't matter who's watching. Just feel it.*

I close my eyes, giving into the moment as I twist my body around the pole before snapping forward to show the audience my ass. Then, I open my eyes and look over my shoulder, giving them a sexy smile before working myself higher until I'm floating on adrenaline.

I wasn't wearing much when I came out here, obviously, but even the act of removing the see-through lace bra and too-short mini skirt feels natural to me.

It's a game. Draw the prey in and ensnare them with your wiles until they're so caught up in you they can't see past it. And it's a game I know I'm winning.

Every now and then, I catch a glimpse of Devlin. He's most definitely ensnared and none too happy about it if the grinding of his jaw is anything to go by. But, the ever-cool businessman he is, he doesn't let it show on his face.

When the song ends, I'm breathing heavily and sweating under the lights, feeling like I've won something.

"Not bad," he eventually says once the music has stopped. He needs to be heard, after all. "I'd like to see how you move to something you haven't choreo-graphed to perfection."

I scowl at him and see his smirk, but I don't rise to the bait. I want this job too much to let my mouth get the better of me in this moment.

"Meaning?" I question, and he stands, moving his chair out from the table before sitting back down.

"Meaning, I need to see how well you can improvise. There will be times you may need to cover for someone else, or a client chooses a certain song." Dammit, he's right. "While you can choose the songs you perform for your scheduled stage routines, private dances are different. The client is able to pick the song," he states.

"Okay, Mr. Thomas," I concede. "What song would you like to see me improvise to?"

He looks shocked that I've asked him, but I get the feeling he would just shoot down anything I came up with, thinking I have other routines lined up.

"Phil!" Devlin shouts, and a man comes over to him.

He's dressed in an all-black suit with an earpiece to communicate with other employees. He's definitely another member of security like Paul is, and he's built just as thick, too.

I have never understood why some women are attracted to the overly muscular type. I know it's a big deal, and I can appreciate the work they've put into themselves to look that way, but I'm more interested in the men who aren't so bulky.

I like my men to be tall and solid but lean enough that I can wrap my arms around them easily. I want them to be strong enough to use me as a rag doll in the sack but not so strong that I feel as though I'm a fragile piece of china.

For me, it's all about balance.

"Yes, boss?" Phil says, and I watch on as Devlin nods to acknowledge his appearance. He's respectful to his employees. I like that. Some bosses look down on the people who work for them, and I hate it.

"Think of a random song and don't say it. I want you to go tell Jazz what it i and have him play it when we signal. Please," he finishes off, and Phil nods before disappearing.

"That's a different tactic," I state, trying to kill some time with chatter, so my nerves don't show.

Devlin smiles. "If you don't know what it is before the music begins, you can't start rehearsing moves in your head that could match the beat." My shock must show because he chuckles, shaking his head. "I read your resume, Ms. Engels. Dance and choreography are a part of you. It would be fairly simple for you to work it out in your head beforehand."

"Interesting. You know a lot about choreographers, boss man?" I sass, and he pins me with a look that has my insides swirling.

He's really damn hot when he looks all serious like that. That look could get me into trouble if I'm not careful.

"This is my business, Ms. Engels. I make it a habit to know everything in order to ensure its success," he states, completely cocky, and fucking hell, it's doing something to my panties.

"Ready!" the DJ, Jazz, hollers, and Devlin gives me a wicked smile.

"Let's see what you've got," he says, and I straighten my shoulders back.

Game on, boss man. Game on.

# 5

# DEVLIN

I HIRED HER.

Shit, how did I let this happen? I have one goddamn rule. Don't stalk my employees. And until now, it's been an easy rule to follow.

I'm a man who focuses on his job when he's here. While the women I hire are attractive in their own right, it's easy to only see them as employees and keep my obsessions away from here.

Until her.

"Oooo, you hired her," Phil says, shaking his head as I walk back into the office.

I have a small amount of time to get my shit together before the club opens. With Shelby starting later this week, it will give me a small reprieve to work through whatever the fuck is broken in my brain when it comes to her.

I can separate this. I can.

"Did you see the way she moved?" I questioned, annoyed to hell that he chose that song.

Actually, I'm not sure if I'm annoyed he chose it or that she passed our rigged test with flying colours. We have a set list of songs to choose from, ranging in genres so that we can test the dancer's skills.

*Sexy Drug* by Falling In Reverse isn't an easy song to dance to on a whim, and dear God, she was sinful as hell.

"Boss," he hedges, "I only followed the rules."

I watch him, wondering why he looks like he's about to shit himself. It's not as though I'm a violent person and he should fear for his safety. I'm not my best friend.

Sure, I can be a hardass when it comes to running the club, but I've never had anyone look at me with this type of fear before.

"I know that!" I snap, unable to take the look on his face. "Why the hell are you looking at me like I'm about to kill your mother?"

"You just look a little... murderous, boss," he points out, and I sigh, dropping into my chair.

"Sorry, I'm just tired." I run my hands over my face before looking him in the eye, making sure my face is calmer. "I had a late night with my best friend last night. Too much alcohol."

Too much alcohol for sure, but I wasn't with Jonathan. No, he's too busy doing fuck knows what lately. So it was just me, myself, and a bottle of Jack… and Jack is an asshole.

He winces. "Right. I'll get her the employee package to fill out so you can relax until we open. Maybe the hair of the dog that bit you could help," he says with a smirk, knowing full well I don't drink when I'm here. Not that I haven't been tempted in the past, it's just not a smart business decision, even if it would take the edge off of this hangover. I need to be alert when I'm here in case shit hits the fan.

Fuck, even the nights I don't come in, I don't drink until after closing to make sure I can be reached in case damage control is needed. Just because we're an upscale business doesn't mean shit doesn't get fucked up every now and again. We deal with skin and alcohol. It's bound to happen from time to time.

"Thanks, Phil. I appreciate it," I tell him honestly, opening the bottom drawer of my desk and handing him a new employee packet.

"Anytime, boss. Need me, just shout."

I nod, and the moment he leaves, I get up and move to the door to lock it. I need a minute of peace, and if my door is locked, no one will bother me unless it's an emergency.

Once I'm back in my chair, I rest the back of my head on the top, staring up at the ceiling.

"I cannot cross this line," I remind myself. "She's my employee and nothing else."

My phone pings, and I lift it up, groaning. It's the background check I've had done to look into Shelby. I always do recon before I begin stalking them, but now it would be unethical to read this. Right?

"Fuck it." I can read it without acting on my obsession. Besides, it will be good to know all I can about her since she's now working for me.

By the time I've devoured the contents of that email, I'm not only cursing myself all over again for hiring her, but I'm also sporting the worst hard-on I've ever had in my goddamn life.

Shelby Laura Engels is a risk taker. An adrenaline-seeking junkie, which probably explains why she sought out a job working here.

It isn't that she necessarily needs the money. Though, judging by her bank account balance, it definitely won't hurt. It's that she wants and needs to feel eyes on her. She wants the high from the attention being on stage will give her.

"Fuck," I groan to myself, tossing the phone onto my desk.

On the one hand, I'm beyond fucking annoyed that I hired her. But on the other, I'm pleased to be giving her something she clearly needs. It does something primal to me to know I'm providing for her in a way.

God, that sounds fucked up.

Knowing this won't go away unless I do something about it, I quickly undo my pants and reach in to pull my length out, hissing when my hand wraps around it.

"Fuck, feels so good." I don't even remember the last time fucking someone felt nearly this good, let alone my hand. Fucking hell, I'm losing my mind.

As my fist grips my cock, I find myself thinking back on the way prairie's hips had moved on stage, wondering how fucking incredible it would feel if she rode me like that.

I pump my cock harder and faster, twisting my fist as images dance around my head, imagining the sounds she'd make as I fucked her hard and rough while choking the goddamn life out of her until she flew apart on my cock.

I can feel the impending orgasm start to build at the base of my spine and start fucking my fist, thrusting my hips into the air and squeezing myself tighter, imagining it's her sweet cunt gripping me as she breaks apart.

My release blinds me, hitting me like a freight train that has me roaring into the office like there aren't people outside in the halls.

Fuck, I've never lost control like this in my life. I can't catch my goddamn breath as ropes of cum continue to spill over my hand and onto my pants as physical proof of my undoing.

When it's finally stopped and I've had a chance to breathe, I take stock of my ruined pants.

My release is everywhere, including the floor, and if she were here and mine, I'd make her lick up the mess she caused me to make. Just the thought of her cleaning everything up with her tongue has my cock thickening again, and I have to put a stop to those thoughts.

I kick my pants off before standing to walk into my ensuite bathroom, cleaning myself up before grabbing a spare set of slacks and readying myself for the night.

Staring at myself in the mirror with a harsh glare, I mutter the only words that come to mind.

"Get over this shit, and remember she's your goddamn employee. That will never happen again."

Yeah. I wish I could believe myself. I'm so fucked.

# 6

# SHELBY

MY FIRST NIGHT has been amazing so far. I've already finished my first set, and now I'm helping the girls serve drinks on the floor.

For a Thursday night, it's really fucking busy. I think I'd feel overwhelmed if I hadn't spent most of my teen years helping out in Daddy's sports bar. Whether it was technically legal for me to be behind the bar or not, no one batted an eye.

We live in a small town of mostly elderly people, so it's not like there was anyone willing to argue the point. While there are always teenagers around town, the majority of them up and leave the minute they graduate high school.

Some eventually come back when they've already

started their families or even retired years later, but the only true consistent in our town is the elderly.

They all knew Dad was and is a good person, but once I turned seventeen, some of the patrons started acting differently around me, and Dad didn't like it. That's when he had me start helping in the back instead. I understood it, but it wasn't necessary. I can handle my own, even back then.

Unfortunately, office and kitchen work aren't my thing—it's too mundane and boring—so I gently told Dad I was going to find another job which he completely understood.

It's actually how Olivia and I started with animals. Back then, we opened up a dog walking service, and it just grew. When we graduated, Liv took courses to become certified in pet grooming, and with her grandma's help, she opened the shop we now love and run together.

Though, if someone brings another dog in that smells like raw fish, I'm going to walk out. Last week, someone had been walking their tiny dog by the pier when it somehow fell into a pile of fish guts. Walking into the back room to that stench is some-thing I'll never forget and something I never want to relive.

"Well, if it isn't Shelby Engels as I live and breathe." The voice instantly has me on edge.

Fuck. Why hadn't I thought about Ben Breton frequenting a club like this? He's a scummy piece of shit, but he's rich. Of course, he'd come here.

I steel my spine before choosing to ignore that he even spoke to me, but I don't get far. The second his fingers wrap around my upper arm, my skin crawls, and fury fills me.

"Don't walk away from me, pretty girl," he taunts, and I whirl to stare him down.

I've hated this piece of shit from the moment I met him. He's Olivia's older brother and has always looked down on her, treating her like trash because she's different. She's kind and sweet and genuine. Everything Ben and his father aren't.

"Get your slimy hands off of me, you cowardly piece of shit!" I hiss at him, wrenching my arm from his grasp, but he just smirks.

"Now, now. No need to be vicious. You liked my touch once upon a time."

My stomach rolls at the reminder. "I was so drunk I didn't know what was happening, and you being the vile asshole you are, took advantage of me. Not once did I want you to touch me," I growl quietly, trying to hold down the bile.

"I don't remember you saying no, sweetness," he taunts, knowing full well he held his hand over my mouth so I was unable to speak or scream.

I'd been sleeping over at their house with Olivia one night so we could drink away from her grandmother's all-knowing look, and she passed out fast. I wasn't nearly ready to just fall asleep, so I got up to wander around.

I was only sixteen at the time, but neither of them were supposed to be home. More often than not, the only time Liv ever went to their house was when she knew that Ben and their father wouldn't be home. But Ben was there that night, at least in the later hours.

"What brought you here? My dear sister not paying you enough?" He sneers at the mere mention of Liv, like she's somehow beneath him.

"None of your goddamn business," I tell him, looking around us to make sure we aren't bringing attention to ourselves.

While I may need Phil's or Paul's help in a worst case scenario where Ben is concerned, I have no intention of allowing it to get that far. I refuse to lose my job on the first night after working so hard just to get hired.

"Well," he says, looking thoughtful as his eyes

rake over my body. "You're not my usual type. Tiffany is most definitely my go to girl." Of course, she is. She looks barely fourteen even though she's almost thirty. Ben has a type.

"Stick with Tiffany." It's a simple statement, but one he doesn't take well. He hates that I've turned him down so easily.

"I don't think I will," he snarls, stepping up to grab my elbow tightly. It takes everything in me not to yelp as I feel my bones rub together.

My eyes scan the crowd again before I look Ben dead in the eye.

"Last chance to get your hands off of me, Ben, before you wind up buried in concrete," I hiss, beyond pissed and ready to kill him here and now.

I would be completely fine with going to jail for murdering him. One hundred percent, it would be worth it.

"I think you mean cement," he says, like he thinks I'm an idiot.

I bark out a humourless laugh. "God, for someone who thinks they're so smart, you are, in fact, beyond stupid," I snark, even as his grip tightens, threatening to break my arm.

Fuck him.

"Clearly, no one has taught you a lesson on how

to shut the fuck up and be a good stripper. I think I'll do that now," he seethes, and I act without thinking.

Lifting my knee, I jam it into his junk so hard he howls loudly and drops to the ground.

"I told you to get your goddamn hands off of me, you sick prick!" I scream, knowing we now have the attention of everyone in the room. If I'm going to lose my job over him, I'm at least going to get some of my anger out.

I move back over to him, stomping on his hand with my five-inch heels until he screams in more agony, loving the sound. I never got the revenge I wanted for him raping me back then, so this is extremely therapeutic.

Until it's not.

"Engels. Office. Now!" I hear Devlin shout, and the look of pure anger on his face when I find him in the crowd is hard to miss.

I'm in so much fucking trouble.

# 7

# DEVLIN

FURY UNLIKE ANYTHING I've ever known courses through my veins as I watch my obsession take down one of my bigger patrons, but my anger isn't directed at her.

If Jonathan hadn't already contacted me yesterday to set up a night where he could get Ben out of here without witnesses, I would go over there and kill the bastard myself for daring to touch her.

*Shit, man. Get your head together.*

"Engels. Office. Now!" I bark out before I can think better of it. The anger is clear as day in my voice, and the moment her beautiful, wide eyes meet mine, I watch as her walls slam up even higher.

Does she think I'm going to hurt her?

*No, but she probably thinks you're angry with her.*

Fuck.

Spinning on my heel, I storm back to the office, not even waiting to see if she's following me. I just need a goddamn minute to think.

"Boss," her voice breaks through my thoughts not ten seconds later, and I internally curse myself.

"Please have a seat," I say, being as gentle as I can while feeling this volatile.

"Considering you're most likely firing me, I think I'll remain standing," she quips.

When I finally look at her, she's standing so stiffly a part of me wonders if it's hurting her to remain that still.

"You're not getting fired," I tell her, sighing as some of my anger drains from me.

Now that she's before me and I know she's safe, I can breathe and think more rationally.

"I'm not?" she asks, looking suspicious. "I just kneed what I can only assume is one of your best customers in the balls before almost crushing his hand."

*Yeah, and it was hot as fuck to see you defend yourself like that.*

"He was touching you against your will. That is strictly against the rules." I zero my eyes in on the elbow that asshole had been holding, and my anger flares back to life.

He held her so tightly she's already beginning to bruise, and it's more than a little swollen.

"You need to go home and ice that," I bark, and she doesn't even jump. Odd. Usually someone who has just been through something like this becomes jumpy afterward.

"If you're not firing me, then why do I need to go home?" she sasses, looking ready for a fight, but I see the way she winces as she crosses her arms over her chest.

"Because it's almost closing time, and your arm is starting to swell. I will not tolerate any of my girls being harmed at work." I shake my head. "I have some logistics and damage control to run to ensure you're all safe," I explain, and she snorts.

"Ben Breton won't charge you for my little outburst."

She does know him, then. That makes this even fucking worse. He's a scumbag I wish I could turn away, but he's never outwardly done anything worth being kicked out for. Not permanently, anyway.

Unfortunately, I have to play politics too, and a move like that without a damn good reason could result in my club being blacklisted with the richer families in the city. Not legally, but word of mouth is a powerful thing, and Ben and his father have a lot of goddamn pull around here. But, given Jon is after him, it's clear Ben has more skeletons in his closet than I'm aware of. Good riddance to the fucker.

"Even if he tried, it wouldn't get far." I shrug, cocky as all hell.

If worst did come to worst, Jonathan's status at the DA'S office, along with his reputation as a lawyer, would help me get out of any type of lawsuit. Not that prairie needs to know that.

"Well, that's good, then," she says, looking like she doesn't believe me for a second, and that makes me want to dig deeper into her possible knowledge of Ben. But I won't cross that line. She's my employee.

If I remind myself enough times, maybe it will stick in my thick fucking skull.

"Please go home and take care of your arm." She looks ready to fight me on it, but I hold up my hand. "No, I won't take you fighting me on this, Miss Engels. You need to go home. I would send any of you home if you were hurt, and you will still receive your full night's pay."

She rolls her eyes at me like the pay isn't something she's worried about, and she's probably not, but I'm firmly in boss mode right now.

"Fine." She huffs, looking annoyed. "You're sure everything will be alright?"

I watch her fidget for a moment as tiredness starts to wash over her. If she were mine, I'd refuse to let her drive home and call her a car, but she would never accept that. Not right now, anyway. Hell, maybe not ever, given the stubborn streak I've seen in her thus far.

"Yes, everything will be fine." I take a second to figure out how best to word what I want to say next. "You did well tonight."

She smirks as sparks dance in her eyes. "Until I took down a jackass."

I bark out a laugh, shaking my head and dropping into my chair to start making some calls.

"Go home, Miss Engels. I will see you Sunday."

She gives me a curt nod before excusing herself, closing the door behind her and leaving me alone.

I close my eyes, breathing through the anger as I replay the interaction between her and Ben in my head.

She was clearly pissed at him from the moment he even went near her, but touching her had been what set her off.

I grab my phone to check the messages from my security team, and breathe a sigh of relief that Ben chose to leave. As pissed as he may be about being taken down by a woman, his bruised ego will never win over his need for women.

It's only a matter of time before he comes back, and Jonathan can deal with him.

# 8

# SHELBY

POOR LIV. Honestly, she finally put herself out there and went on a date, just for the guy to be a sleaze. Now I feel bad for even suggesting the dating app to begin with.

To make matters worse, Ben was the catalyst that pushed her into accepting the first date she'd been asked on. I'm sure he was taking his anger out on her as a way to get back at me for making him look bad. Not that he needs an excuse. He hates his sister, but it's rare for him to reach out like he did.

For as long as I've known them, he's done his very best to knock her down at every turn. Telling her she's fat and worthless, calling her a pig. He's always been a mean son-of-a-bitch, and he gets it from their father.

I hate that he taunted her and made her feel so little that she sought validation from the first man to show her any form of affection. Well, the first man other than this Carmichael guy.

He'd come into the shop to adopt a dog the same day Ben texted Liv, and the moment she left, he turned into this cold asshole. It was completely different than the way he had been treating Liv while she was there.

Then, I went ahead and flirted with the asshole like I didn't just swear off one night stands and random hookups. The guy is attractive, but he's not my type. I don't know why I hit on him in the first place, but it was clear my advance wasn't wanted.

"Why was he there tonight?" I ask myself while driving the car home.

I made a joke with Olivia about him being uptight with my flirting, acting like I was completely saddened he turned me down. But if I'm being honest, only one man has my eye right now, and he's off limits.

Could it really just be a coincidence that he was there to step in and intervene tonight? To get that guy off her back? Probably, but it still feels odd. I'm sure I'm just being paranoid from watching too much true crime tv, though.

Ha! There's no such thing as too much crime tv, but seriously, I am definitely overthinking this.

Besides, the guy is a hot-shot lawyer. If I'm going to be worried about anyone hanging around her, it's the asshole she went on a date with.

As soon as I get home, I shoot off a text to Liv to let her know I made it safely before going inside. She is such a mother hen, but it's one of the things I truly love about her. It just adds to her charm.

"Shower, wine, bed," I remind myself, getting to work on that list because tomorrow is a double shift kind of day, and I'm fucking tired.

* * *

"Hey, blondie," Beth calls out to me as I make my way toward the back rooms.

She's an older woman and scary as hell. She runs the bar with an iron fist, and I've never seen one customer trying to fuck with her. She has a reputation, and word has it the bat leaning in the corner isn't just for show.

"Hey, Beth! Good to see you in tonight!" I wink, and she scoffs.

"I practically live here, kid."

I chuckle and keep moving. We're about to open,

and I'm the second dance tonight, which doesn't give me a lot of time to change and do my makeup.

"Hey, Cherry! How are you doing tonight, girl?" one of the girls asks me.

They started calling me that when my opening act was a schoolgirl outfit with pigtails, dancing to *Cherry Pie* by Warrant. I'm not even mad about it. With my long blonde hair in pigtails and a sexy as fuck skirt that is way too short for anything other than selling sex, damn right I'm willing to wear that name with a badge of honour!

"Hey, Red," I greet her.

Everyone here goes by their stage name in case anyone is around, but most of these women are like sisters. They share everything about their lives, and I wish I was a part of it, but I'm the new girl. One day I will earn their trust, but I've been here less than a month. There's a lot they don't know about my life, and I'm not sure I ever want them to, so I can't exactly expect them to divulge their innermost secrets.

By the time Tiffany's number is up, I'm ready to go on stage for my routine, deciding to use the dance that gave me the name Cherry. It is one of my all time favourite songs, and it's sexy as fuck to move to. But more than that, I think I saw Devlin blow a few blood vessels that night.

Adrenaline is pumping through me as I walk onto the stage, hoping the boss man will be watching. I don't know why I enjoy riling him up so much, but I can't bring myself to care either.

The music starts playing, and I grab the pole with one hand, slowly swinging around it before dipping down low and tossing my head back to show the crowd my barely covered chest.

The hoots and cheers drive me wild, spurring me on as the song continues.

Letting go of the pole, I hook my thumbs into the sides of my skirt, twisting my hips in a way that has my ass grinding against the pole. I can't see anything past the bright lights, but I like to imagine some of them groaning.

I wonder briefly if Devlin is groaning, aching for relief for his cock.

*Whoa, Shelbs. Slow the fuck down. You do not need to get wet while you're up here.*

I twirl my hips back and forth, slowly lowering the skirt until it's passed my bare cheeks, then let it drop to the ground. Making a turn on with the toe of my shoe, I double fist the pole, stroking it like I would a giant cock before smirking and bending forward to shake my ass at the crowd.

More barks and cheers fill my ears as bills land on the stage by my feet, the men and women showing me just how much they love what I'm doing to them.

When I stand back up, my eye catches someone standing by the corner of the stage, just out of sight from the people watching, and my heart rate kicks into high gear.

With my back to the majority of the lights, I can see the boss man watching me, a feral and predatory look on his face that makes my pussy clench.

Fuck, that dominance is just so goddamn hot. It's time to see if I can make more than a few blood vessels pop.

*This is for you, boss.*

I blow him a kiss before turning around, taking the tight white shirt off and swinging myself onto the pole, dropping myself backward so my tits sway with my body, making sure he gets a good eyeful along with everyone else.

# 9

# DEVLIN

I'M GOING to ban that goddamn song. Prairie is a damn tease. I know she saw me watching backstage last night, and now the image of her swinging around almost naked is seared into my memory forever.

I still refuse to stalk her. It's a line I'm trying desperately not to cross, but it's hard. Though, I suppose I'm stalking her at work, so I've already technically failed. I just refuse to acknowledge that right now. As long as I keep it within the confines of this building, I'm only blurring my rules, not flat out obliterating them.

"You wanted to see me, boss?" Beth says from my office door, grouchy as ever. I don't take it personally. She's like this with everyone.

"Yes, thank you. Come have a seat," I stand up to greet her, respectful in any way I can be.

If I'm being honest, Beth fucking terrifies me. I've seen the older woman break up bar brawls between six guys completely by herself. And not at our club. Once in a while, some of us like to get together and go out for drinks. One of the bars we landed at— thanks to a now ex-employee that is rotting in prison for shit I don't even want to think about— was a shithole.

I'm talking warm beer, too crowded, and filled with some people that watched us like we were scum on the bottom of their shoe. Look, I'm not a snob, but that place was just not it.

Beth didn't seem as uncomfortable as the rest of us and insisted we stay to have a few drinks, so we did. When a brawl broke out around us, with the now ex-employee, Beth jumped in the centre, almost giving me a fucking heart attack, but she schooled the six men like nothing I had ever seen in my lifetime, and now I have massive respect for the woman.

Respect and a healthy dose of well placed fear, because you do not want her on your bad side. Whatever happened in her past, it was definitely dark.

"What can I do for you, boss?" she asks, sitting down and giving me a look of respect. I appreciate the respect my employees give me, but it never ceases to amaze me because I feel like I don't do enough for them.

I know several of my girls are here because they need the money. That if there was any other option for survival, they would have gone down that avenue instead. Not everyone is like Shelby and seeking a thrill, but they never complain, and they know they're safe working for me. Unfortunately, in Chicago and the surrounding area, there's just not a lot of work to be found, especially without a degree.

It's sad to say, but even being outside of the city like we are, there aren't too many paths for people who are desperate to survive. I'm just thankful I can help the girls I do, giving them enough to survive and thrive for themselves and their families.

I've seen more than one girl leave here thinking she had a better offer just to find out she'd been added to another tragic statistic. A fallen victim of the ruthless streets of Chicago.

"How is the newest hire handling the floor?" I ask her. I know the answer already because I know everything about that woman when she's here in my building. She's doing incredibly well. This is definitely not the first place she's served drinks before.

"She picked it up real quick. Only fuss she's made at all was the night she took that rich guy to the floor," she states, a smile skating across her face.

It's no real shock that Beth is proud of Shelby for taking care of herself and making the asshole pay. I don't think I've ever seen Beth warm up to any new hire as quickly as she has Shelby. Then again, we don't exactly have a lot of shit like that happen around here.

"She wasn't reprimanded for that," I tell her, shocking myself with how open I'm being.

Beth watches me closely for a moment, not giving anything away. "Something there the rest of us aren't privy to?" she questions me, and I sigh.

"Something is definitely there, but I don't know much more than you. Even if I did, it would have been told to me in confidence," I remind her, and she nods. Though I can see she doesn't believe me.

"He was here last night," she tells me like she thinks I wouldn't know.

"I know. Paul and the rest of security are keeping a close eye on him from here on out, and he's been issued a warning about keeping his hands to himself.

If he pulls another stunt like that again, he's out." But he won't have the chance.

I doubt Jon will take much longer to make his move now that the prick has come crawling back to the club. He's planning to make his move in a couple of days when Tiffany is back on shift and Ben is guaranteed to be here. And personally, I can't wait to never see the fucker again.

"Good. He's always given me the creeps," Beth states, giving an overdramatic shiver.

"Why the hell didn't you say something before now?" I bark at her, not meaning to raise my voice at her.

She snorts, shaking her head and standing. "I know how the real world works, boss. I know there are a lot of politics involved with these richer-than-God pricks. One opinion from a little old lady doesn't mean shit."

I blink, letting her words sink in.

Does she actually believe her word has no weight here? I can't have her thinking that when she's proven time and again just how solid her intuition is.

Standing, I straighten the suit vest I'm wearing and meet her eyes, making sure she sees the truth reflecting in mine.

"If there's something off to you, at any time and about anyone, I need you to tell me, Beth. You've been working for me for a long time, and I completely trust your intuition. If someone is bad news, we can make sure to watch them more and keep the girls safer together. Yeah?"

Her eyes shine with admiration and surprise before locking back down. She gives me a quick nod, and heads toward the door.

"Sure thing, boss. Gotta get back and set my bar up before the shitshow begins. You need anything, let me know."

Oh, I need a lot of things. Unfortunately, Beth can't give me any of them.

# 10

# SHELBY

I LOVE TRUE CRIME.

Seriously, Liv and my parents have voiced their concern for my sanity on more than one occasion, but I just can't get enough of it.

I love learning about cases, reading about and analyzing the evidence, and ultimately finding out who the killer is. When it comes to watching true crime tv or reading books on solved cases, ninety-eight percent of the time I can tell you exactly who the killer is before the big reveal. But my favourite kind of crimes to read and watch are cold cases.

There's just something about knowing these were the killers that did something different and were never caught, you know? It challenges my mind to analyze the evidence and see what makes each case different from the ones where the killers were inevitably caught.

Sometimes I don't see a difference, and it gives me hope that they will eventually be caught for the crimes they've committed. Other times, there's a clear indication that the killer put more forethought into forensic countermeasures in order to get away with it.

I'm not naive, either. I'm fully aware that there are more killers out there than will ever be caught. Even with the advancements in forensics, there are still far too many that will always get away with it because law and forensics are, and will always be, largely based on human capability. And humans, as a whole, are very much prone to mistakes. That's just the harsh reality of this world.

I open my iPad as someone walks into the shop, but after a moment, it's clear Liv doesn't need me. Whoever came in must just be booking an appointment for their dog and not looking for a walk-in appointment.

I open my browser, instantly going to Chicago's largest online newspaper, and scour the articles.

The world is really fucking depressing. After a few minutes, I come across an article that has my heart racing as disbelief clouds my mind.

Is that…? No. Can it be? Holy shit.

"Oh, my fucking GOD!" I screech, jumping up from my chair like my ass is on fire. "Liv, what was that douchebag's name again? You know, the one who tried to get all up in your lady business last week!"

I hold my breath, staring down at the picture while I wait for her response. It fucking can't be.

"Uh, I'm busy, Shelbs," she answers, loud enough for me to hear.

Oh, she's most definitely not too busy for this!

Grabbing my iPad off the table, I practically run to the front of the shop, stopping dead in my tracks at the sight before me.

That lawyer I tried to hit on is standing very close to my best friend, and I don't like it. Not one fucking bit if this article is about who I think it is. "Oh," I say, trying to keep the anxiousness out of my voice.

Olivia gives me an odd look. "Jonathan came back to look at the dogs available for adoption at the local shelter!"

She's so happy that it diffuses some of my anxiety. Not a lot, but a little. Enough that my head snaps back to the current situation at hand.

"Cool. But seriously, what was his name again?" I

look between them before settling on my bestie's face.

She looks at me like she's extremely bored and would rather talk about anything else, but this is important.

"Jeff, something. We didn't exactly exchange last names." She winces, barely enough to be noticeable, but the lawyer dude behind her picks up on it, and he doesn't look happy about it.

It's an interesting reaction from a man that doesn't really know her. "Right. Is this him?" I ask, turning the iPad around for her to see.

I see in her eyes the second she recognizes him, and warning bells start blaring in my mind.

"Yeah, why?" she asks, but I can see something dawning on her. She knows me too well to not realize it's nothing less than murder if I'm this excited about it. Like I said, I love crime.

"Because he was just found brutally murdered in his home," I tell her, looking at Jonathan with new interest. He was there that night, too. "It's a good thing you were there. If something had happened to her, I think it would kill me."

Emotion claws at me at the mere thought of something bad happening to my best friend, and I bat away the lone tear that escapes me.

"I'm glad I could be there. What are they saying, though? That's not a common occurrence around here. That feels like more of a Chicago thing," he says, looking annoyed to be having this discussion.

Why, though? Unless he wasn't there by accident that night, and he's been following my best friend.

*No, that's insane. I'm paranoid, right? Maybe these shows are catching up with me.*

"Oh, my God! You're trying to get away from work, and this probably isn't helping," Liv gasps, looking at him like she's so fucking sorry.

"It's okay, I'm just surprised by it is all," he explains, reaching his hand to rub her back in a calming gesture.

Someone who could kill Jeff in cold blood like this couldn't possibly be that gentle. Right? Even if that move is way too fucking intense for someone he doesn't know.

"Apparently, they have absolutely no idea who did it. They can't find a lick of forensic evidence, according to the article," I feign excitement.

If he is the killer, which is probably ridiculous, it's not like I'm going to give away my suspicions. Nope, I'll play the long detective game and wait him out. Assess him from afar.

Olivia groans, shaking her head. "Not now, Shelbs."

Good, she bought it. If I can fake out my best friend, a stranger is a piece of cake.

I pout, pretending to be sad before responding. "Fine. Do your doggy adoption thing and make that golden heart of yours happy so we can make my dark one giddy later!"

Once I give them both a final look, I head back into the room to listen in on their conversation.

He asks her about my dark heart, and she explains my love of true crime. I kind of wish she hadn't done that. It's like waving a red flag over my head that says "Yeah, bud, I'm onto you!" if he is the real killer.

They're quiet for a moment after some small talk before he speaks again, and my best friend's voice sounds happy.

"That's Sadie," she says, and I don't have to be looking at her to see the smile on her face. She fucking loves that dog, and I wish she'd adopt her already. Their connection is just kismet.

"You feel very strongly about her." His voice snaps me out of my thoughts, and I realize I missed part of the conversation, but the moment he insists on her being the one to adopt, I frown.

Why? That is the ultimate question now.

Why did he just happen to be outside of the same restaurant that night?

Why is Jeff dead? Killed brutally in his own bed with no forensic evidence whatsoever.

And why the hell is this extremely busy lawyer insisting on adopting a very traumatized dog that, even to his own admission, he knows my best friend is very attached to?

There are so many questions that need answering. I just need to figure out how to go about it.

# 11

# DEVLIN

He's here.

Ben Breton is like a cockroach that won't fucking die, and I hate having him in my club now that I know there's some sort of past with Shelby. My prairie girl. But the fucker won't be here again after tonight.

Jonathan is already waiting by the back rooms, ready to kill this piece of shit for hurting his woman. He thinks the bastard is the missing link to whoever put the original hit out on her, and he's determined to figure it out before someone puts out a second contract, endangering her and Shelby both.

Jesus, we're both insane.

He's out here killing people for hurting the woman he's claimed as his own, even when she doesn't know she's been claimed. All while I'm here, handing the same bastard over to him without issue for hurting *my* woman.

We're both fucked. The fact that we've each fallen into an obsession with two best friends is ironic, to say the least, given our own close friendship.

I taught my best friend everything he knows on how to stalk a person without being caught, and now he's using those abilities to stalk a woman instead of his future kills.

I'm oddly proud of him for that.

When I see Phil walking Ben toward me, I take a deep, calming breath to make sure I come across as the cheerful club owner who appreciates his business.

"Mr. Breton," I greet, holding out my hand for him to shake it. "I'm so glad you're back."

The lie tastes sour on my tongue, but he smirks.

"What happened isn't a big deal. Shelby and I go way back," he states, and it takes everything in me not to choke him.

Now that I'm aware this prick is Jon's girl's brother, I'm not surprised. I am, however, curious exactly why Shelby had that negative of a reaction to him. It seems like something more personal than him being a shit brother to her best friend.

"I have a surprise for you," I say cheerfully, and he looks confused.

"A surprise?" He's suspicious, but I know he'll go for this.

"Yes. As a token of our appreciation for your business, Tiffany is all yours for the night. On the house, of course." I'm laying it on thick, but he's just drunk enough to not recognize that.

Ben's eyes light up with lust, and I know I've got him. "Lead the way," he says, clapping his hands together and licking his lips.

"I'll take him back, Phil. Just guard the hall and make sure Tiffany is the only one to come back."

He nods, knowing full well Tiffany isn't even on tonight. My men are good at their jobs. They've signed non-disclosure agreements, so what happens at the club stays at the club. Anyone who may come searching for Ben after his disappearance won't get any information from them.

Even if my men had straight moral compasses, our girls come first, and Ben tried to hurt one of our own. They'll never try to save this asshole.

"Is Tiffany already back here?" Ben asks as I lead him to the room at the end of the hall.

He clearly didn't hear what I just said to Phil. He's obviously drunker than I thought.

"She'll be back to join you in a few minutes. She's just finishing up her break so she can spend some extra time with you, one on one," I tell him.

"Why are you being so generous?" Ben asks. His suspicion back.

Obviously, making up for his embarrassment isn't reason enough for him, which ideally, it should be. My woman made him look like an incompetent fool.

I snort. "I'm not. It's Tiffany's birthday, and I told her she could have whatever she wanted as a present. She said she wanted some alone time with your dick." She'd never say that, but it's enough of an excuse to make him complacent.

When we walk into the room, I shake my head as I look him up and down. "Not sure what all the fuss is about, but I'm not going to deny the birthday girl. Are you?"

Ben chuckles. "Hell, no. And sorry, mate, but you're not my type."

When I give him a disgusted look, he laughs harder, and I really just want to get away from the weasel. Heading to the door, I turn to address him once more before I leave.

"Right. There's some of your favourite scotch on the table. First glass is on me. You drink more than that and it's going on your tab." It's the last thing I say before stepping out and closing the door behind me.

Jonathan steps out from the shadows. If I hadn't taught the bastard everything he knows, he would have scared the shit out of me.

"That didn't take long." He's watching the door, and I shrug.

"He's a horny bastard who wants to get his dick wet. It never takes them long," I tell him.

We shoot the shit for a moment, and I'm curious whether or not Jon is going to wait for the drugged scotch to kick in before trying to grab him, but Phil hollers for me from the end of the hall before I can find out.

Once I've told him to hang on, I turn back to Jonathan. "The cameras are set to turn back on in ten minutes. Make sure you're out of here by then."

He just nods, and I turn, making my way to check on Phil. "What's going on?" I question, following him toward the bar.

"Some guy tried to steal a bottle of whiskey from Beth. She has him pinned to the bar by the neck," he says, and sure enough, she does.

Beth has her baseball bat over the guy's neck, holding him down while he kicks and screams. But no one will help him. Anyone who isn't new knows Beth is not one to fuck with.

"What happened?" I ask her, barely giving the man she's holding a glance. I do, however, nod at Phil to take the asshole off the bar and hold him.

Beth sighs, looking tired before her eyes meet mine. She watches me a moment, then nods like she sees whatever it is she's looking for.

"I was getting a round of drinks for one of the girls when this guy kept bothering me." She glares at the idiot in question. "I told him to wait, but he's impatient and a little wild. I don't think he was sober when he came in, if you know what I mean," she says, and I nod.

He was high on something before he got in here. Either that, or he snuck something in and snorted it once he arrived. Probably the second option considering my men are trained to tell when someone is high, and if they are, they're not allowed entry.

"Noted," I say, urging her to continue.

"You told me to tell you if something is off," she says matter of factly. "I'm not saying this because he's high and tried to steal from my bar. Nor am I saying it because he's a little dickhead with no respect," she huffs out, making me smirk.

"Understood."

She grabs my arm and pulls me to the side, out of earshot from everyone else around us and whispers, her eyes filled with a coldness I've never seen from her before.

She looks kind of like Jon does after a kill when he hasn't had a chance to torture them or hasn't felt quite enough to ease the bloodthirst inside him.

"Without saying a goddamn word about my past or my knowledge of the darker shit in this world, that boy is no good."

It's all she needs to say for me to know she's telling the truth, and I promised her I would act on her instincts.

"Phil!" I bark, nodding at her in thanks.

"Yeah, boss?"

"Take his ID and put him on the banned list. No one tries to steal from me or treats my employees like shit."

"You got it, boss man."

Beth's eyes shine with respect as my words sink in, but rather than saying anything, she just smiles and nods, straightening herself up and heading back to work.

I scrub a hand over my face, feeling fucking tired, before checking my phone.

JON:

It's done. Thanks.

I sigh in relief.

ME:

Not a problem. Anytime.

# 12

# SHELBY

"WHAT THE HELL do you mean Ben is missing?" I ask my best friend the second I arrive at her place.

She called me half an hour ago, freaking out because some officers had just left her house after not so subtly accusing her of being involved, and I hate that for her.

Liv is hands-down the sweetest and most gentle person you will ever meet. There's no way she could be involved in her brother's disappearance. Fuck, he's probably just holed up somewhere high as a kite, fucking some poor woman, and ignoring his phone.

So why do I feel like it's something a lot darker than that? First that asshole date of hers, and now her brother has been supposedly missing for a few days? It's suspicious as fuck.

"I mean that they think he's missing." She shrugs, chugging more wine right from the bottle.

I wish I knew how much she's already had to drink so I could watch her a little better. My best friend is a lightweight.

I scoff, tossing my purse onto the counter and taking the bottle from her, throwing it back to try and catch up. When I'm satisfied I've chugged enough to gather at least a little buzz, I hand the bottle back to her.

"We both know he's probably off half-fucked somewhere and hiding from your father." I watch her, and she doesn't react. "He's not really known for being prompt, Liv."

She sighs, nodding and polishing off the bottle. "They also brought up my date with the asshole that was killed," she says quietly. "It's weird, right? For two things to be connected to me?"

"Yeah, it's weird, but so are a lot of things in life, babe. We both know you'd never hurt a fly, so they're not going to find anything to bring against you," I promise her.

Even if I have my suspicions about who may be

behind this, no one would ever believe me. Hell, I'm not even sure I believe me.

"I need more wine," she says, opening the fridge and grabbing another one.

"Just how many bottles do you have in there?" I lift an eyebrow at her, and she shrugs.

"I don't know. A few? People keep gifting them to me, and I don't usually drink, so I keep them in the fridge. Though, they're starting to take up a lot of space."

I smile wickedly at my best friend, opening the fridge and pulling my own bottle out. I don't care what brand or flavour it is, as long as it gets us drunk enough to forget this clusterfuck that's stressing her out.

"Then let's make some space, babe!" I say cheerfully, and she laughs, clinking our bottles together

This is going to be a fun night.

**DEVLIN**

Jonathan is pouting as he heads my way with the presumably dead guy hanging over his shoulder.

Telling a serial killer not to kill someone in a way that leaves blood is like telling a kid they can't have candy before dinner.

When he called me to say that both of our women were getting drunk tonight and asked me if I wanted to tag along in keeping an eye out, I took him up on the offer. I stopped giving a shit about my rules after he came to the club to grab Ben a few days ago.

When we realized that our women were best friends, he pointed out that my rule of not stalking my employees wasn't going to work where prairie is concerned. Not if my obsession with her was anything like his for this Olivia woman.

Prairie. Fuck, she's beautiful, and the obsession is definitely all-consuming. And she was almost hurt tonight because she's too drunk to hear someone breaking into the house.

I guess whoever put out the original hit on Olivia decided to send another killer after all, proving Jonathan's theory that Ben is connected to it all somehow or another. He's only been missing for a few days and suddenly there are more, less trained, killers trying to take her out? It's clear Ben is a part of this.

We're going to have to keep a close eye on these

two whenever they're together. It's not healthy for two women to go through so many damn bottles of wine in one evening, and they're going to feel it tomorrow.

"Here," Jon grunts, tossing the idiotic asshole into the trunk where I've prepped the plastic sheet so no DNA can be recovered from the trunk. "Let's go get our women."

I shake my head, pinching the bridge of my nose in frustration. "Just how am I going to explain to Shelby how she's suddenly at home when she fell asleep here? Not to mention the fact that her best friend isn't going to be reachable?" I ask him, and he sighs.

"Use her phone to call the club, but extend it to your personal line. Then leave a long voicemail that you can later delete." I blink at him. "Make her think that she called you because Olivia had insisted on drunk dialling me. Say Olivia invited me over, and Shelby decided she wanted to be anywhere but here but was too drunk to call anyone else. Maybe say she called you to try and hook up."

Fuck, he's way too clever at this shit. It's like he's thought of every possible scenario. I know I taught him everything I know, but his paranoia as a killer has made him even more dangerous.

"Right. How do I get her back to her place without her waking up? She's drunk, but she's going to remember shit," I tell him.

He smirks, pulling two tiny syringes from his coat pocket, and I hate him so much right now. "With this."

"No. We're not drugging them!" I hiss, and he looks about ready to knock me out and toss me into his trunk with the dead guy.

"It's that, or we risk waking them up and freaking them out. Or we leave them here with the possibility the next killer won't be a novice."

Fuck him and his goddamn logic. Fuck!

"Fine. Let's just get this shit over with before we're seen."

"That's what I thought. Let's get our women," he says, handing me the syringe and heading back into the house.

Here we fucking go.

# 13

## SHELBY

UGH, no. Should have brought whiskey and avoided that fermented grape shit.

Whiskey, I can handle, but fake, wannabe alcohol always fucks me up.

Trying to sit up, my head spins like I've never had a sip of alcohol in my life, and it's confusing me because I can hold my own against a group of tough bikers when it comes to drinking.

There is no way this is from that fucking wine alone.

"What the hell happened last night?" I groan, opening my eyes to take in my surroundings. "That's... not right," I whisper.

I know for a fact I went to bed in Liv's spare

room, so how the fuck did I end up back at my house?

Maybe I'm still drunk and dreaming. It wouldn't be the first time. But no, this isn't a dream. I never feel like this when I'm dreaming, and I feel like complete and total shit right now.

A sound from the living room has me freezing in place, instantly making everything in my body ache and my stomach roll.

Who the fuck could be in my living room? And how the hell did I get here? Nothing is adding up right now.

I need to figure out what's happening, then call Liv to make sure she's okay.

Gently standing, I quietly make my way to my dresser and the hammer I have hidden behind it. A girl can never be too careful, after all. I have a knife under my pillow as well, but with the state I'm in, a hammer is heavier and easier to cause damage with.

I bend down and feel around for it, pulling it to me before standing again.

I do my best to be silent as I open the bedroom door and head down the hallway, stopping just outside of the living room entrance to listen.

Nothing but the sounds of someone snoring greet me, so I look around the corner and see my flower vase on the floor where the sleeping intruder must have knocked it over with his arm.

Thank fuck it's plastic and there's no water since they're fake flowers. A mess of broken glass and water is the last thing I want to tend to with this wild hangover.

Raising the hammer over my shoulder, I make my way to the couch, my heart racing as my stomach rolls from the fear and adrenaline.

God, I hate feeling like this. It feels like I got high on E or something, and I haven't done that shit since I was eighteen. I wouldn't have done it last night, either. Liv is one of the main reasons I never got addicted to any of the drugs I experimented with back then.

She helped me sober up from a fairly bad trip that had scared her, and made me promise to stop. She's my best friend and watches out for me, and I would never break a promise to her.

"WHAT THE HELL?!" I screech, hanging over the asshole sleeping on my couch.

"What?!" He jumps up into a fight stance, his eyes wide as they scans the room before they land on me. "Fucking Christ, prairie! Are you insane?!" he bellows.

"Am I insane? AM I INSANE?! You broke into

my house and slept on my couch, you nut-job!" I screech, waving the hammer around.

"So you decide to hang over my head with a hammer like you're about to bash my skull in?!"

"I didn't know it was you!"

Something darkens in his eyes as he prowls toward me, getting into my space. He grasps hold of my hand grasping the hammer and squeezes while his free hand circles my waist, walking me back until I hit the wall behind us.

"You have random men just waking up in your house on the regular, Shelby?" he asks, his voice deadly.

The audacity this prick has! "Maybe I do, boss," I hiss out his name, narrowing my eyes at him. "That is really none of your goddamn business!"

He pushes harder against my body to make sure I can't get away from him, and it does strange things to me. If I weren't battling the hangover from hell or a possible drugging, I might actually climb him.

"There won't be any more men, Lo," he growls, and I'm taken aback for a moment.

"Who the fuck is Lo?" I question. Jealousy twirls inside my gut, making me angry.

He smirks down at me, his eyes dancing with delight. "You. Your middle name is Laura. It just came out without thought, but it suits you," he says with a shrug.

Why don't I believe that?

Deciding I need to change tactics, I square my shoulders and glare up at the asshole.

"Why are you here? Actually, why the fuck am I here? I know for a fact I didn't fall asleep in my own goddamn bed," I growl out.

He smirks, which just pisses me off even more.

"You called me. It was hard to understand everything that came out of your drunk mouth," he says with a dark look before continuing. "Something about wanting to hook up." He looks deep into my eyes. "I don't appreciate being treated like a booty call, prairie."

My heart seizes in my chest as I try to think back on the night before. The last thing I remember is me and Liv stumbling down the hallway to the bedrooms, both of us completely wasted.

"No," I say quietly, trying to fight the fog in my mind.

I can believe I'd called him for a drunk hookup. I've done worse things while drinking, and this celibacy kick I've been on the past couple of weeks has been horrible.

"I wouldn't leave Liv like that," I tell him in a determined voice.

He scoffs. "She wasn't exactly alone. By the time I was leaving with you, you were passed out, but someone was pulling into her driveway." He smirks then. "He didn't seem to like seeing her as drunk as she was. Guess he cares for her quite a lot."

So many possibilities fly through my mind. What if it was her father? God, that man could have hurt her, and Devlin wouldn't have known any better.

"What did he look like?" I question, grabbing his shirt in my fist, ready to beat it out of him if necessary.

"Tall. Probably in his forties with dark hair."

My panic settles a little before ratcheting up a few notches.

If what he's saying is true, that would mean Jonathan was there. I would never leave her alone with him if I wasn't passed out. Not when I believe he's a potential killer, for fuck's sake!

"You did." He pulls away, releasing my hand from his shirt, and takes his phone out of his pocket, tapping on it a few times before he shows me the call logs.

If I believe what I'm seeing, then there's no reason to think he's lying. But calls can easily be faked and manipulated to fit any narrative if you're willing to go to that length.

"Where is Olivia?" I snarl, any semblance of calm now long gone. Like I said, a call can be faked.

I rip the phone from his hand, dialling her number, but it goes straight to voicemail. After ten attempts and no answer, I feel like I'm going to throw up as I begin pacing.

"She's safe, I'm sure."

Maybe he thinks this will calm me, but it won't. He'd probably think she was if he knew the man was a lawyer, but he's also a murderer. I know down to my core that I'm right about him.

"She'd never call a guy over," I state firmly before turning on him and stomping over to where he's standing. "And I feel like I've been drugged. I know for a fact I stopped doing drugs, so nothing is adding up."

Something akin to anger passes his eyes. It's gone before I can fully understand it or call him out on it, though.

"You're not thinking clearly right now, prairie," he says the condescending, yet sweet, nickname in a way that reminds me of trying to diffuse a bomb. "You were wasted when I arrived and passed out before we got to the car."

"I'm sorry I tried to have sex with you," I say with a frown. It's entirely plausible if I was shitfaced enough. And Devlin is exactly my type, so I can see it happening.

"Hey, I'm not complaining," he says with a laugh.

"You're not the first guy I've tried to hook up with while drinking," I admit, as much to piss him off and get under his skin as it is to remind myself it's possible.

"I don't like that," he snarls, and I roll my eyes, deciding we need to change the subject.

"Where's my car?" I question then, realizing the obvious answer is that it's probably at Liv's still.

"It's still at your friend's house. I can take you to get it once you're ready," he says, holding his hands up in a placating gesture.

"Just let me get dressed." I huff out a breath and stomp off to the room. I'm not going to argue with him if he's willing to take me over. It's quicker and easier than trying to grab a cab, and I definitely don't feel like walking right now.

It only takes a few minutes to throw on some yoga pants and a hoodie before I'm back in the living room, where he's waiting for me.

"Drink this. Take these," he grunts out the orders and shoves a water bottle and some ibuprofen at me.

I will not swoon at this. No fucking way. I kind of want to, but there are way too many unanswered questions right now.

Throwing the pills back, I chug the entire bottle of water before giving him a nod.

"Let's go. I need to see her."

# 14

# DEVLIN

She's fucking livid.

After I dropped Shelby off at her car, I pulled away and rounded back on foot to keep an eye on her as she practically tore Olivia's house apart. She was clearly looking for her friend or anything that could lead to answers.

Answers I knew she wouldn't find.

When she realized there was nothing to be found, she got into her car and drove home. I followed—obviously—at a distance I knew she wouldn't see me, and she's been pacing around her house ever since.

Honestly, I'm amazed she hasn't gotten tired or dizzy yet, given the hangover from hell I know she's dealing with.

When she brought up being drugged, I almost lost my shit. I didn't want to drug her in the first place, but Jon was right. We needed to get both of the women out of there quickly and quietly, meaning we had to drug them.

I didn't realize my prairie girl had a past with drugs, though. That very well may have changed my mind about how things went down last night, but it's too late to go back now.

She doesn't seem to be spinning out of control looking for a fix like someone who had fallen off the wagon would, so that eases my mind a bit.

I watch as Shelby moves away from the living room window again. When she's out of sight, I open the camera feed on my iPad while dialling Jonathan from my phone.

"Hey, you good?" he asks me with a laugh.

"Define good. I got the crazy bitch home and stayed with her until she woke up. She came at me with a goddamn hammer," I hiss, my memory flooding back to the panic that set in when I opened my eyes this morning.

Jonathan laughs. "Sounds perfect for you," he teases, and I sigh.

"She really is. Anyway, I gave her the story that she'd called me drunk off her ass for a booty call." I hate lying to her, and that's a first for me. Lying usually comes easily. "She apparently buys that part just fine. Not sure whether to be happy about that or hire you to kill all the bastards she's slept with in the past," I grit out, making him chuckle again.

Asshole.

"Be happy she believes you," he reminds me. "What about Olivia?" He needs to know where Shelby's head is at with her best friend currently in the wind, which isn't something Olivia would do on her own.

"Oh, she's already losing her shit, not being able to get a hold of her," I tell him with a smirk. "I've been watching her all day, and she's a ball of fury. What do you want me to do?"

"Call her in for a double shift or something," he tells me. "Make up an excuse of needing her at the club. I need you to buy me some time. I have to wait until Liv is sobered up before I can talk to her about everything, and hopefully have her message Shelby from a cloned phone."

I laugh, knowing he's in for a fight if she's anything like my woman.

"Are you sure she's not going to try and cut your nuts off the second she realizes you've kidnapped her?"

He groans. "I doubt it will be easy, but I will do whatever I have to in order to protect her. I'll make her see that her friend's life will be in danger if she asks too many questions."

My man has it bad. Then again, I'm not one to talk.

"Good luck, man," I reply, hanging up once he says 'you too'.

I watch the iPad. Shelby goes into the kitchen to finally make something to eat, and I ponder what to do.

There's always the choice Jon gave me about calling her into work, but I don't think that will work for either of us tonight. She definitely needs to rest, and her mind won't be able to focus at work until she hears from Olivia anyway.

Settling onto the ground behind a tree, I pull out my wireless earbuds and put one in so I can listen in on her. I need to see where her head is at.

\* \* \*

**SHELBY**

. . .

If he thinks I can't sense him outside of my house, watching me, he's wrong.

I am far too on edge about waiting to hear from Liv, so my senses are working overtime right now.

I know it's Devlin, the big boss man, watching me and not someone else because it feels the same way it does at the club.

Hot, dirty, and filled with a sort of possession he refuses to act on. At least, not yet.

Taunting him with each dance I perform has become a favourite game of mine. I'm always learning new routines and moves to drive him absolutely insane while I'm on the pole. It's just a bonus that I get incredible tips at the same time.

When I started working for him, I thought my adrenaline and need to be seen would be fuelled by the customers, and it is to an extent. But the best high I get is watching him lose his goddamn mind as I show myself off.

Now that I've had something to eat, I need to do something to take the edge off, and I know just the thing.

Moving into the living room, I strip off my clothes before walking to the curtain. I close it enough that it looks as though I'm vying for privacy, but I purposely leave it open for him to watch me.

When I saw a flash of something behind the tree across the road earlier, I just knew it was him. At first, I was furious and almost stormed out there with my hammer, but I decided I'd rather play.

After all, he did toy with me this morning, getting all growly and pushing me against the wall over the idea of other men in my house. Turnabout is fair play, right?

Once I have the curtains perfectly situated, I strip off the last of my clothes and move to the chair across from them to sit down.

I keep the smirk off my face by sheer will as I lift both legs to drape over the arms of the chair before moving my hands to play with my tits.

The pleasure that rips through me as I squeeze and toy with my nipples—accompanied by this show of exhibitionism—has my clit throbbing in record time.

I can feel myself getting wet as I continue to play until a moan escapes me. When I can't take it anymore, I move one hand down to my centre, whimpering as my finger expertly grazes my swollen clit.

"God, yes," I moan, moving my finger to circle the outside of my clit before putting direct pressure on the bundle of nerves.

"Oh," I cry out, my hips lifting off the chair from the zing of arousal shooting through my core. "Fuck."

It feels so good like this. Hotter than it usually is, knowing he's watching me.

I abandon my other breast and move my hand past the fingers on my clit, settling at my entrance.

I'm already so wet and needy, I'd kill to ride a cock right now, but this will have to be enough.

Sliding my fingers through my folds to wet them, I move back to my entrance and slowly push two inside of me.

"Yes," I moan loudly as my pussy clenches around my fingers.

"Fuck, fuck, fuck," I pant and whine in time with the thrust of my fingers as my other hand works my clit until I'm screaming my release at the top of my lungs.

"Yes! Oh, God, yes!" The orgasm tears through every part of my body, leaving me taut and breathless while I ride the high. I can feel how soaked I am, and I know I've left a mess on the chair to clean up. I don't even care.

"Holy fuck," I whisper when I come back down, gently removing my fingers from my channel and bringing them to my lips to taste myself.

It's not something I'd do if I was truly alone, but if I have to be horny because he's watching me, then he can feel my pain by being so goddamn hard he can't sit down.

The idea of him sitting out there, hard as a rock and dying to touch me, gets me hot and bothered all over again.

It only takes a second before I decide to go another round and get myself off once more, but this time, I'm imagining his cock being forced down my throat while he pulls my hair.

When I cum again, I scream out another man's name just to fuck with him, hoping it will force his hand. He *will* be the first one to make a move.

# 15

# DEVLIN

CHAD? Who the fuck is Chad?

God, my dick is so hard it's going to bust through my goddamn zipper. Her screaming another man's name isn't even enough to tamp down the desire coursing through my body.

"I'll kill you, Chad. You motherfucker," I hiss, pulling my phone out and searching through the deep dive I had done into her life.

After five minutes of searching, I come up empty. There is absolutely no Chad in her life. Past or present. Which means she's playing me. She knows I'm watching her.

Interesting.

My sweet and fiery prairie girl can sense

someone watching her. More than that, she can sense it's me.

I know for a fact she feels and sees my eyes on her at the club. I make a habit of always being there when she is because if even one goddamn customer tries to grab her the way Ben did, I will make sure their bodies are never found.

Before my best friend became a serial killer, I was a skilled stalker. The best. I taught him everything I know about stalking, and he taught me how to kill without ever being caught.

Him being a lawyer for the DA's office is definitely a bonus. I never intend to kill anyone or anything outside of insects because it's not who I am, but my protective obsession over Shelby knows no bounds.

"Take that, boss man," Shelby says, drawing my attention back to the iPad.

She's smirking toward the curtain that she had closed most of the way, and it's clear now that it was a deliberate move on her part to leave it partly open.

Fuck, now I'm even harder for her. I'm losing my God damn mind.

Okay, this doesn't change much. She still doesn't know about the cameras in her house or the fact that

I've read all of her diaries and know every intimate detail about her.

Wow. This is one of those times where I wonder about my own sanity for a split second before deciding I don't give a shit.

I think it's about time to stop pussyfooting around Shelby with this obsession and finally make my move. Though, I'm going to have to wait for her friend to call her before I can, but that will happen soon. I know Jon, and he won't let anything happen to someone so close to his woman. My obsession just makes her that much safer.

Shelby is as safe as she could ever be, and we'll make sure of it.

I watch her move through the house, naked as fuck, and the need to relieve some pressure is almost too great. But I can't do that with her. Jerking off behind a tree across the street while I watch her on a camera just feels... wrong when it comes to this woman.

I want to save all of this cum for her. When I finally get her on her knees for me, I want to blow this load all over that perfect, fuckable face.

"Oh, Shelby. You've unlocked a beast in me, baby. You want to play games and be a brat? I'll play along for a while." I smile into the night as I watch her climb into bed for a mid-day nap. "I'm coming for you, prairie. Get ready."

* * *

The sound of Shelby gasping in shock and fear pulls me back to the video feed on my laptop. The iPad is currently charging in the back seat, but I always have eyes on her.

Since the ground isn't exactly comfortable, I moved back to the car when I realized she wouldn't be waking up anytime soon.

I hate that she's been so off today because she's worried about her best friend. I hate that everything had to go down the way it did last night, but it was the only way. At least she got some rest.

"Olivia fucking Breton, you better tell me where the fuck you disappeared to on me!" she screams into the phone.

I can feel my eyes widen at the tone she just took with Olivia. Jon is not going to like that, best friend or not.

I shoot him a message, telling him to breathe— because I know for a fact he's going to be pissed— before focusing back on Lo.

She jumps out of bed and starts pacing the room like she's on a mission as she listens to her best friend on the other line.

"Oh yeah? Then how come I can't use find a friend to see where you are?" Shit, she's smart as fuck. I wish the other two luck getting around that one.

"What? Why would I judge you? That seems stupid."

More silence and pacing.

"Liv, who did you call? I know you didn't call Ben, since half the reason we got wasted was because the fuck-tool is missing."

Fuck, just that prick's name on her lips makes me furious. I have to remind myself that Jon is handling it.

There's another small gasp of shock and Lo stops pacing.

"Say what, now? You messaged the hot lawyer with a stick up his ass?" she asks, completely dumb-founded and making me laugh.

Their conversation goes on for a few more minutes before Shelby hangs up.

While she looks mollified for now, I have the feeling this conversation is far from over. When my phone dings and I look at the text from Jonathan, I know I'm right.

JON:

You know I'm going to need to speak
with her in the near future.

Yeah, I know. I hate it, but I know.

# 16

# SHELBY

Liv has been staying with that lawyer Jonathan for a few days now, and I don't like it.

I'm at work with her often enough to see she's not suffering, but I don't trust the man. The way he watches her is unhealthy, especially if he's the one that killed her date and took her brother.

And if he is, I hope he kills that bastard and makes it hurt. He deserves anything that comes to him, but I still don't want that kind of negativity around Liv.

I know I don't have a lot of room to talk given how my boss and I watch one another, but I feel like that's different. Boss man and I are a little wild. Olivia really isn't. She's the most docile human being

I have ever known, so this intensity between them feels out of place and foreign.

She's falling hard and fast, and it's really fucked up. Not to mention she messaged me this morning to tell me she was keeping the shop closed today, then I hear about shots being fired down the road?

I know she's safe since she didn't go into work, but fuck. I don't like anything that's been happening recently. Shit like this doesn't happen in our town, and nothing is adding up.

"Evening!" Beth hollers at me from the bar as I walk into work.

I smile over at her and wave before moving to the back room. Devlin messaged me earlier saying I had a private dance booked just before close, and I'm a ball of nerves because it will be my first one.

For whatever reason, he hasn't let me take on a private session yet, citing the probationary learning period and such. There have been several requests made, so maybe he's tired of fielding them off. Private dances don't just give me more income, the club makes a lot of money off of them as well.

"Hey, Cherry!" Tiffany greets me when I walk through the door to the back.

She's a nice girl. Although, she never used to talk much. I don't know if she didn't talk much because I was so new, or if she's just opening up more because Ben hasn't been around lately. I have a feeling it's a mixture of the two, but I'm glad for the company.

"Hi, Tiff," I say back, forcing a smile I really don't feel right now.

"Rumour has it you're getting your first private tonight." She's smiling at me, but I can see the strain in her eyes. "If they do anything wrong, don't hesitate to call security, okay?" Her voice cracks a little, and my heart aches for her.

Knowing the type of man Ben is, I bet she didn't have a chance in hell at calling security. I should talk to the boss man about having a better system in place if that's the case. Then again, maybe she was unable to say no to Ben because she needed the money that came with his cruelty. Either way, I wish things had been different for her, and I hope that bastard is never found.

"I promise you, I will scream like a banshee if they try anything." I wink, and she laughs.

"You can if you need to, but boss man has help buttons hidden throughout the room. Screaming is a last resort if you're being held down, and I really hope that never happens to any of us."

That is something we can both agree on.

"Someone would have to be awfully stupid to

cross Devlin Thomas like that," one of the other girls says as she walks in behind us.

"It happened once," Tiffany says, and that has my attention.

"Someone has held a girl down before?" I ask in shock.

"Yeah, a few years ago. Apparently, the dancer screamed so loud that everyone heard her over the music." She shudders. "Security got there just as the guy dropped his pants."

Holy shit.

"Yeah. That's when Devlin hired the top security firm in the country to man the club and added even more cameras and emergency buttons into the rooms," the other girl says as she sits down in front of the mirror to do her makeup.

"Holy fuck," I whisper, and Tiffany nods.

"Yeah, but the guy is lucky security got there first because Beth was on their heels with a sawed-off shotgun. No one even knew she had it hidden behind the bar. He was seconds away from having his brains splattered all over the walls."

Yeah, that tracks with what I've noticed about Beth. She's very protective over us and this place. Sometimes I wonder if she spends even more time here than Devlin.

"That's insane," I acknowledge as we spread out to do our own makeup to prep for the night.

"Things are a lot better now. Most of the patrons know to keep their hands to themselves, but you can never be too careful," Tiffany says. The slight hitch is still present in her voice, but I refuse to call her out on it. We all have our stories, and I can understand hers with Ben more than she knows.

"Alright, ladies!" Jazz, the DJ, claps his hands at the door. "Give me those playlists! I need to make sure everything is perfect for you to rock out tonight!"

Jazz is sweet and hilarious and completely gay. It doesn't feel nerve-wracking when he's in here like it does with some of the security team. It's not even that they're scary, because we all know they would never lay a hand on us, but they're intimidating as fuck.

Large and fucking in charge. Jazz often feels like one of us girls rather than another man in our lives.

I hand my paper to him, and he leans down to kiss my cheek before moving to the next girl and doing the same.

Once he's exited the room, I grab my makeup from my purse and start applying the shit on thick.

I absolutely hate wearing makeup like this. It's so

heavy and unnatural to the touch, but it's stage makeup. No matter how much we sweat up there or while serving drinks, this shit stays put.

"Fifteen, Cherry!" one of the guards yells through the open door a while later.

I didn't realize so much time passed already.

"Got it!" I holler back in acknowledgment before grabbing my bag and heading to the bathroom to change.

I hope it's busy tonight. Anything to keep my mind off this private dance later will be a blessing so my nerves don't get the better of me.

# 17

# DEVLIN

"Absolutely fucking not," I tell Jon as I pace the floor of my office.

"I told you I would have to speak with her," he says calmly.

I'm aware of that, but I didn't know he was going to threaten her when we decided on the private dance as the time to do it. Now that we're half an hour away from go-time, I've changed my mind.

"You can't threaten her!" I snap, and his eyes widen in shock before his face shuts down completely.

"She's putting Olivia at risk while waving a red flag over her own head that will draw that bastard to her. Do you really want him to go after Shelby if she doesn't keep her mouth shut?" he says coldly.

I've been in the room with this version of my best friend before. Many times. But this is different. His coldness is directed at the woman I think I'm fucking in love with, and I will not let him hurt her. Not that he would physically, but I know he's going to scare her tonight.

"Who wants your woman dead?" I ask, moving to sit back down in my chair across from him.

"Her father."

I blink. "You're certain?"

He nods. "I am. I killed Ben tonight, but I made him sing like a fucking canary first." The rage covering Jonathan's face is palpable as he works his jaw.

"That's fucked up," I respond. "Why the hell has he put a hit out on his own daughter?" Which in turn endangers anyone she's close to.

Fuck.

"I hope to have some answers tomorrow after I take her back to her place for some things." He shakes his head. "You can't stop me from confronting Shelby, Dev. I know you love her, but I love Liv too, and Shelby is putting them both at risk by looking into things that are better left alone."

Dammit. I know he's right, but that doesn't make it any easier to swallow.

Prairie is going to hate me after this, and call me love-struck, but I've been enjoying this dance of wills the past few days. We haven't said a word to one another, but it's clear we're playing some kind of game, and I have no idea who's winning.

I could lie and say I am, but I know myself well enough to know that she has me beyond trapped in her net. She's in charge of the game, but I'm about to win it.

One thing this night will do is bring the pussy-footing to an end. After tonight, she will know I'm best friends with a killer, and all bets will be off. That's when I'll make my move, because I'm done waiting.

Employee or not, Shelby Engels is mine, and she's about to know it too.

"You're right. I just don't understand how any father could stoop so low. How does one find justification in having their own child murdered? And for what? There is nothing in the world that is worth killing your own flesh and blood over. Not anyone like Olivia, anyway," I state, my stomach rolling just thinking about it.

"He's a sociopath." Jon shrugs. "They don't have the ability to feel human emotion."

"Aren't you a sociopath?" I question, and he rolls his eyes at me.

"No. If I were, you'd be dead, and I wouldn't love Olivia the way I do," he points out like he's bored. "I'm a neurotic individual with psychopathic tendencies. That means, while a lot of my actions mirror those who truly are psychopaths, I can still feel human emotion." He shrugs as a smirk crosses his face. "I just happen to be overly selective on who I give a fuck about."

That's putting it mildly. Fucking hell, the man has never shown an ounce of love to anyone outside of Olivia since we were kids. Well, I guess maybe me, but we don't do the lovey-dovey emotional shit. It's not really our style.

"I'm not sure I will ever understand how you operate," I say with a smile.

I do understand it. As well as I can, at least. He's always had a darker side to him growing up that no one else saw. He didn't go around killing animals or any of those other precursors most serial killers have, but there has always been something deeply rooted inside of him that made him different from the rest of us. Something darker than most of us could ever fathom.

"You know exactly how I operate," he replies with a dark chuckle.

An alarm pings on his phone, and I know our time is up. He's about to confront my prairie girl, and I have to help him because she needs to listen to what he has to say. And if he doesn't get through to her, I will do everything in my power to make her see reason.

"It's time." He shoots me a look, and I nod in acknowledgment, letting him know I'm not going to fight him on this anymore.

"Don't hurt her," I state as I stand up. I know Jonathan doesn't hurt women, but I needed to say it as much for my comfort as it is a reminder to him how much I care for her.

"I'm not about to garner the wrath of my grand-mother's ghost, and you know women are off limits. Women and children are my hard limit in this job."

I don't point out that his first kill was actually a woman. Not just because he wasn't the one that stabbed her a dozen times and left her to die, but because it doesn't matter.

Jonathan Carmichael would never set out to intentionally harm a woman or child, and that woman he found bleeding out would have suffered far longer before she died if he hadn't strangled her with her own scarf. The medics never would have made it on time, and he knew it.

"I know, Jon. I know."

"She's safe regardless of how frustrating she is to me. Olivia would never forgive me if I allowed any harm to come to her best friend."

I stop and look at him for a moment, studying him. "Where is Olivia right now? Does she know you're here?" I ask, and he smiles as a lustful look crosses his face.

"She's passed out, but I need to make this quick. I don't want to be away from her for longer than absolutely necessary. I want to be holding her when she wakes up."

Damn, he's so whipped. I'd make a joke about it if I wasn't in the same damn boat.

"Let's get this over with then."

# 18

## SHELBY

"ARE YOU ALRIGHT?" I ask Devlin as we head into the hallway where the private rooms are located. He seems exceptionally uptight and on edge, and it's freaking me out more than I like to admit.

"What? Why would you ask me that?" He grimaces when I give him a dull look. "I'm fine, just a bit stressed. Don't worry about it," he says, stopping in front of a door and turning to me.

"Right," I say, tilting my neck side to side to shake off my nerves.

"You ready?" he asks, looking me over like he isn't sure I can handle what's about to happen.

"I could say something corny like 'I was born ready!' but that seems idiotic." He barks out a laugh and shakes his head, unknowingly relieving some of the nerves inside of me. "Yeah, I'm ready."

He nods and opens the door, standing back to let me walk inside. When he steps in behind me and closes the door, I turn back to face him, but his eyes are on the patron waiting for me in the room.

When I was first hired, I was given a tour of the club, so I know behind me is a fairly basic room. There's a small stage in the corner with a pole, a sound system set up beside the stage for our performances, and a black velvet bench that runs along the entire wall facing the stage. But none of that is as important as the look on Devlin's face as he stares at the stranger who clearly needs my attention.

Turning back around to meet the patron, my heart beats faster when I see who's standing on the other side of the room.

"Shelby." His voice is dark and cold as he says my name.

"Jonathan," I say, trying to match his cold tone. It's not that hard, considering what I think of him. "Sorry to burst your bubble, but I refuse to dance for you."

I know he's not here for a dance, but I feel the need to stand up to him. Even if it gets me killed.

"We need to talk," he tells me, and I laugh dryly. Yeah, sure we do.

"I'll guard the door," Devlin says behind me.

Whirling around, I glare at him. "You're going to leave me here with him?" I question, and he nods.

"You need to listen to what he's saying to you, Lo." He looks at the murderer behind me. "They're closing the club down now."

"Good. Thanks," Jonathan says behind me, and I grab Devlin's suit in my fists, standing on my toes to get right in his face.

"What the hell is going on here, boss man?" I seethe.

"Jonathan is my best friend, Lo."

Holy fuck. He's in on this? All of it?

"So, everything you said about the safety of your girls was bullshit," I hiss, and his eyes widen.

It should be noted that he hasn't tried to touch me or pull away from my hold of him.

"He won't hurt you. That I can promise you."

Before I can react, he grips my wrists in his hands and pulls me hard against him, moving my wrists quickly to pin them against my lower back.

"Don't you ever question my loyalty to you again," he snaps out a split second before his mouth is hot and demanding on mine.

He presses harder on my hands to force my body even tighter against his, eliciting a moan from me before I realize it. Devlin's mouth tastes better than I ever imagined, and I *have* imagined it. I've imagined how all of him tastes.

With that shocking reminder, I gasp and tear my mouth from his. "Get your hands off me, boss man, before your dick ends up as bad as Ben's," I hiss, but my choice of words is clearly a mistake.

Devlin spins my body around and presses my chest against the door, leaning in to whisper in my ear. "You're going to pay for that," he snarls.

There's something fucked up about me, because this show of control does nothing more than piss me off while turning me on. Fuck, he's so goddamn hot.

"Never compare me to that waste of life again, prairie," he snarls, pulling away from me so fast my head spins.

Quickly gathering my composure, I turn on him with a blank face before looking at Jonathan. "You want to talk to me? Fine, but your little bitch boy can toddle off now."

The murdering asshole that has my best friend's heart smirks, shaking his head with a chuckle before nodding to Devlin, who growls.

"I'll be right outside." Devlin looks between us for

a moment, clearly unhappy, before stomping to the door.

As soon as the door slams shut, Jonathan takes a menacing step toward me. He's not the first devil I've tangoed with, and if I'm about to be killed, I refuse to give him the satisfaction of seeing my fear.

"It's pretty ballsy of you to provoke him, considering he's the one that gets to choose when you leave this room," he taunts, and I snort.

"I can handle him just fine. I've dealt with assholes before." I stare him down as he slowly circles around me to stand at my back.

"I am very much aware of the things you've been through," he says quietly.

Just the way he says it tells me everything I need to know. Some way, somehow, he has discovered the one truth that I never wanted anyone in the world to know. Least of all, Olivia.

"So it was you," I state, proud that my voice doesn't waver.

Jonathan hums behind me. "What was me?" he asks, and I hate that he's playing with me. He knows I know.

Turning around and taking a few steps back to get away from him, I look directly into the devil's eyes.

"Don't play with me. We both know why you're really here." I guess he's not the only one playing games since I won't say it aloud. If I do, it makes the fact that I'm about to die much more real.

He smiles like he realizes what's going through my mind right now.

"I can assure you I am not here to play any sort of game, Shelby," he says, moving fast as he pushes me back against the nearest wall.

From here, it's easy for him to tower over me. He looks down at me like he's a predator ready to charge his target. But as scared as I may feel, he will never fucking see it.

"Then what the fuck do you want from me?" I hear the small shake in my voice at the end and silently curse myself. Any hope that he didn't catch it vanishes when I see the sadistic smile on his face.

"I want you to stop sticking that nose of yours where it doesn't fucking belong," he snarls, that smile dropping in a split second.

I actually snort. "Good luck with that."

He growls, punching his gloved fist through the wall directly beside my head, making me jump.

"No. I mean it, Shelby. This fucking ends right here, right now. You will stop looking into my past and into anything to do with the current events surrounding Olivia."

"The current events surrounding her?" I ask innocently before snarling in his face. "Oh, you mean the guy you murdered because she went on a date? Or do you mean the fact that her brother is also missing, leaving her smack dab in the middle of an investigation and making her the prime fucking suspect?!" I scream.

He curses before pushing me harder into the wall with his proximity, still careful not to touch me. "So, you have me all figured out, right?" he taunts, his voice low and threatening. "Did you know that bastard she went on a date with has a history of raping underage women via manipulation?" I swallow as he continues. "Or how about the fact that he tried to rape another woman later that night at a bar. Hmm? Did you know that?"

I whimper, my fear finally getting the better of me. Liv was only on that dating site because I pushed her to do it, and she could have been hurt because of it.

"I didn't think so. And how about Ben? Do you really think I would allow someone like that to exist in her life? Someone who continues to hurt her so deeply?" he questions, and I shake my head slowly as he ends his speech. "I know what he did to you when you were sixteen."

"No," I whisper.

"Yes."

"You... you can't say anything to Liv. Please, I don't care what you do to me, but please. Never tell her what you know," I beg him, my heart breaking at the mere thought of my best friend finding out her brother raped me when we were teenagers.

"I would never tell her that. It's your secret to bear, and nothing good comes from dredging up the past." He shakes his head.

"How?" I don't look at him as I ask how he knows the truth.

"Because I made that bastard tell me his deepest, darkest secrets as I tortured him to death slowly for what he's done to my sunflower," he growls out, and my eyes shoot up to his.

"You killed him." It's a statement, not a question, and he knows it.

"Damn right I did. I also killed the little prick that called her a fat cow a while back." He smiles like he's enjoying the memory. "His vile tongue was the first thing to go for daring to speak to her that way."

Fucking Christ. This man is unhinged.

"And now you're here to kill me."

He rolls his eyes at me like he's bored. "I'm not here to kill you, but I am here to warn you. You need to back off."

"She deserves to k—"

"She knows," he says, cutting me off and shocking the hell out of me. "In fact, she knows a hell of a lot more than you do, so I need you to open your goddamn ears and listen to me. Understand?"

He pulls back to give me a bit of space, but not enough that I could make any form of movement that might be seen as threatening.

"Yes," I say quietly.

If Liv truly does know all of this, then she's chosen to stay with him willingly. I know Olivia. If he was holding her against her will, he'd have scratches and bruises all over his face from at least trying to escape.

She may be docile and sweet, but she's also incredibly strong-willed. She would never go down without a fight.

"Good." He breathes out a sigh of relief. "Long story short, I came into Olivia's life because someone put a contract out on her." I'm going to be sick. "The second I saw her picture, I knew she was the only woman for me. I vowed to protect her from harm." He takes a steadying breath.

"Ben was the key to finding out who was behind it, but when he disappeared, the person put out another contract. I stopped them from killing you both the other night and knew she had to come back to my house in order to keep her safe."

"Shit." Things start making sense in my mind.

He nods. "Then someone tried to kill her today. If Sadie hadn't started growling, Liv and I would both be dead right now."

"Liv!" I cry out, but he ignores me.

"That's when I went back to the house and finally got the answers out of Ben that I needed before killing the slimy bastard."

"Who? Who wants her dead?" I rasp, and he looks me dead in the eye.

"Her father."

# 19

# DEVLIN

"ARE YOU FUCKING KIDDING ME?!" I hear Shelby screech through the door.

Enough is enough. Jonathan has had more than enough time to make her see reason, and I'm done fucking waiting.

When I push through the door, Jon is standing in front of her, but there's a good distance between them. Lo is pacing the floor, looking more pissed off than I have ever seen her, and I find myself glad there's not a hammer in sight.

"That low-down, good-for-nothing son of a bitch! I'll kill that bastard myself for even daring to try and harm her," she snarls.

Jon looks toward me and rolls his eyes before

casually checking his watch. "My sunflower has been asleep for a while now, and I do not want her to wake up alone." He looks back at me. "She knows the cliff notes version of everything. You can fill in the blanks later, but I need to go."

He walks toward Shelby, taking her shoulders in his hands and halting her pacing. "You will not do a goddamn thing. Olivia is my woman, my love and soul, and mine to protect. I'm a trained killer, Shelby. I promise you that man will breathe his very last breath soon enough. I just need to make sure it doesn't come back on Olivia. Stay. Away."

With that, he releases her and walks out of the room, closing the door behind him.

"Prairie," I say, my voice husky. I've been hard from the second my lips touched hers, and her sheer defiance only solidified her fate tonight.

Shelby Engles is about to be mine.

"You knew he wasn't going to kill me?" she snaps, still heated at everything she's just learned.

"Of course I did. Do you honestly think I would allow you to be anything but safe? No one will ever hurt you again."

She tilts her head and scans my face for a lie she expects to see but won't find.

"You led me to a room with a fucking serial killer, Devlin!" she shouts. Thank fuck everyone is already gone, or else she would be drawing attention to us right now.

"One that vowed to never hurt you," I tell her, stepping closer.

"Sure," she scoffs.

Once I'm before her, I grip her chin with my hand, bringing her face closer to mine.

"I've known him most of my life, Lo. He doesn't hurt women and children. Even if he did, you happen to be very important to the only two people he cares about on this earth. You are completely safe." I smirk. "From him."

Her pupils dilate, but instead of giving in to what she wants, she fights me.

"You're on my shit list, boss man."

"Oh, prairie, that's half the fun," I admit before lowering my mouth to hers.

I kiss her hard, tightening my hold on her chin as I lift it to push my tongue past her lips once more.

The whimper she lets out before her tongue meets mine in a battle of wills sets my soul on fire.

Biting her bottom lip before chasing the sting with my tongue, I delve back into her mouth. She may be kissing me back, but she's still standing as still as a statue, refusing to give in to me so easily. I know she wants this just as badly as I do.

"Bad girl," I growl into her mouth. Dropping her chin, I move both of my hands into her hair, fisting it at the roots and pulling tightly.

"Don't kid yourself, boss man. You don't want a good girl," she taunts, and fuck me. It is the sexiest thing I've ever heard.

This. This is what I've missed with every other relationship I've been in. Every obsession I've ever had. The fire. The back and forth fighting for dominance. But it's more than that. It's her.

I was waiting for her.

"Say you're mine, prairie," I grunt against her lips, kissing her hard one last time before pulling away.

"I don't belong to anyone," she sasses, and I fucking love it.

"Wrong. You belong to me, and we both know it." I lower my head and start kissing her neck.

"I know no such thing, boss man."

I gently bite below her ear, and she gasps before her hands finally move to grip my forearms.

"Oh, prairie girl, the things I know about you," I tease, chuckling against her neck. "You've been mine from the moment you stepped into my goddamn club with that holier-than-thou attitude."

I trail my lips down her neck, allowing the tip of my tongue to poke through as my hands leave her hair and move to her waist, pulling her tightly against me.

"Shit," she moans, the sound going straight to my dick.

"That's it," I praise when she pushes her fingers into my hair.

"Me giving into you doesn't mean you own me," she snarls. It turns into a moan when my teeth graze her collarbone.

"I don't want to own you, Shelby. You're not an object." I pull away from her to look into her eyes, but all I see is confusion.

"So, it's just sex then?"

Not a fucking chance, baby.

"Never," I promise with conviction.

"Then what?"

"This? Us? It's not ownership. It's obsession. I don't want to own you. I want to possess your goddamn soul as much as you do mine. You'll never get rid of me, baby." It's a threat I plan on keeping until my dying breath. And by the look in her eyes, she knows it too.

"Interesting concept," she says with a smirk. "Don't I get a choice in this?"

"You made your choice the first time you screamed my name with your fingers buried deep inside that sweet cunt."

## SHELBY

Cocky much?

"That's an awfully bold assumption," I sass. With each passing second, I'm becoming more addicted to this back and forth game of ours.

"I'm not assuming anything. I. Know," he states, looking smug as fuck.

He may have correctly guessed that I've gotten myself off to thoughts of him more times than I can count, but he doesn't know shit.

"There is no evidence backing up your claim," I reply confidently.

He chuckles, shaking his head. "You were wearing a silky pink slip that left nothing to the imagination." Oh fuck. "You spread those beautiful legs of yours apart. Then you moaned from the feel of the air on your cunt as you toyed with your nipples until you were writhing on the bed sheets."

My brain and body are frozen from desire as he leans in closer, spinning a tale I know all too well as truth.

"But you still didn't play with your cunt. No, you decided to torture yourself, running your hands all over your body, lighting every nerve ending on fire," he says, his breath grazing my lips.

"Stop," I whisper, rubbing my thighs together.

"When you finally did touch yourself, you were dripping with need." He leans in and bites my lower lip with a growl. "And you came screaming my name, prairie. Mine!" he snarls before kissing me hard.

He moves us back, his tongue tangling with mine like he's angry at me for not admitting how badly I want him. We move until I feel the bench hit my knees, and he pulls away.

"You have cameras in my house," I growl through my lustful haze.

I should be pissed off at the complete invasion of privacy, but I'm not. It suits us. It fits with how obsessively he watches me while we're at work and how he stalks me at home, even with how I taunted him instead of calling him out.

It's perfectly right for our story.

If I had given it any thought, I would have known there were probably cameras inside, but I was too busy toying with him every waking moment I could.

"Yes." He isn't ashamed of it, and that confidence just makes me hotter.

"I should castrate you," I hiss, but he smirks.

"You aren't even the slightest bit angry. It turns you on, knowing I've been obsessed with you from the start. That I can't stop watching you every second I'm awake."

He can read me too well, and I'm not sure how to feel about that.

"Just how many women have you done this to?" I ask, quirking a brow. I straighten my shoulders and sit down on the bench, letting him tower over me.

I'm not afraid of him, and he doesn't have the upper hand, even from this position.

"They don't matter because you're the last. You are officially the only woman I will stalk for the rest of my life, prairie. Congratulations," he taunts, but the darkness swirling in his eyes is proof enough that he's telling the truth.

"I possess you?" I ask, switching gears.

Just the idea of him stalking other women has me

ready to gut any bitch he's ever laid eyes on, and that is not where I want tonight to go.

His eyes flare with heat as he leans down to be eye level with me. "To the very depths of my soul, Lo." His nostrils flare. "You're buried so deeply I'd never get you out, even if I wanted to."

But he doesn't want to be rid of me.

"Mmm." Running my hand up his chest, I curve it around the back of his neck and squeeze, licking my way up his cheek before whispering in his ear. "I believe you told me I was going to pay for a certain comment I made earlier."

He grunts, pulling himself away enough to wrap his hand around my throat, making my breath hitch.

Fuck, why is that so hot?

"Tell me you're mine, Shelby. Tell me I possess you as much as you possess me, and I will give you everything you want," he says, watching me closely.

I want to. Fuck, I want to, but it's terrifying. "And if I don't?" I ask, my voice cracking when his hand tightens and cuts off some of my air supply.

"Then you don't get to touch me until you come to your senses. And I won't touch you, even if you fucking beg me."

My eyes flare with anger, but I smirk. "I haven't

needed you before, boss man. I am fully capable of finding release in other ways."

His hand squeezes impossibly tighter as he lifts me by the neck and brings my face to his. The move is so dominating that my pussy floods and soaks my thong while coating my thighs even more.

"If you even think about letting another man touch you, Jonathan won't be the only murderer you've met," he snarls. "I've never killed a man, but I promise you I know every one of his tricks."

I swallow against his grip, my eyes starting to get blurry, but it only makes me needier for him.

"Try me, prairie. I dare you." His voice snaps me out of my thoughts.

I open my eyes to look into his, nodding my head enough that he lets me go. I drop back to my feet, gasping for air. His hand never leaves my throat, and I find his touch grounding me even as I fight to fill my lungs.

"If you're mine and only mine, then yes. I'm yours," I tell him, moving my hand to cup his hard length, giving it a hard squeeze.

He sucks in a breath when my grip gets uncomfortably tight, but his eyes are dancing with pleasure.

"But make no mistake, Devlin. I will fight you

every goddamn day on everything you try to control me on," I promise, and he laughs.

"I wouldn't want it any other way," he grunts, grinding into my grip. He's a lot bigger than I originally thought he was just from looking at him, and I'm dying to play.

"If you so much as look at another woman, my stalker, I will slit her throat in front of you before killing you too." His dick jerks against my palm, and I smirk. "I'm not going to give myself to you just to be hurt, so be careful. You may have just signed your own death certificate."

## 21

## DEVLIN

THERE'S no doubt in my mind that she was made for me.

"If claiming you means I signed my own death certificate, then I will die a happy man, prairie," I tell her truthfully as I grind my cock into her fist.

It's killing me to have layers between us. I want to feel her throat filling with my cock until she can't breathe, and she was promised a punishment. But I also deserve a damn reward for holding back from her this long. It's about time she screamed my name because of what I can do to her.

"Rest your back against the bench," I order. Releasing her neck, I pry her hand off my cock and groan.

"Why should I do that?" she sasses, heat sparking in her eyes.

She's so fucking wet for me. All I can smell is her, and I need to have her taste on my tongue before she swallows my dick. I doubt she'll tell me no, either.

"If you want me to clean up that sweet mess soaking your thighs, you'll do as you're told, prairie. Be my naughty girl and lay back."

She swallows her desire and walks backward, bending down to pull her thong off her legs slowly. My mouth goes dry as my heart races, knowing she's about to submit to me.

Fuck, I've wanted this moment for so long. Now that it's here, I feel like I'm in some kind of altered state. Like this isn't real, and I'm going to wake up with my hand once again wrapped around my cock.

"You're going to clean me up?" she asks, her voice raspy as she sits on the bench and looks at me.

"What do you think?" I quirk a brow, moving toward her.

She leans back with a smirk, biting her lip. "I think you want to make me even dirtier."

Fucking hell.

I groan, palming my dick through my suit pants before kneeling on the floor in front of her, her scent filling my nostrils and making my mouth water.

"Oh, I plan on making you filthy, prairie, but not just yet."

"You're all talk and no a—" she stops talking the second I grab her knees and pull her toward me so her back thuds against the bench.

"Oh God," she whimpers as I forcer her knees apart, taking in the sight of her drenched lips before me. I'm so close I can almost taste her.

"Not God, prairie. But when I'm finished with you, you'll be worshipping my cock." It's the last thing I say before sliding my tongue up her thigh, tasting her sweetness that coats them.

"Fuck, baby," I growl. "If tasting you this way is so delicious, I'm a doomed man. Your pussy is going to be my new addiction." I bite the top of her thigh hard, making her gasp in shock.

"Devlin!" she shouts, and I chuckle.

"Already screaming my name," I tease, shaking my head.

"I'm scolding you," she says breathlessly. "It doesn't count."

Growling, I move and nudge my nose into her sweet cunt, inhaling deeply. "Scold me all you want to, but it still counts."

The smell of her is too much to handle, and I can't hold back any longer.

"Oh," she whimpers when my nose nudges her clit.

"Hold yourself open for me," I demand, refusing to let go of her thighs now that they're over my shoulders. When she goes to say something smart, I move my hands down and dig them into her ass cheeks to leave my mark.

"Asshole," she grumbles, but moves to do as I demand.

"Good girl," I groan in praise when she's fully on display for me. "Fuck, you're perfect, prairie."

"If you don't put your mouth on me right this second, I—"

"You'll what?" I ask, blowing cold air onto her clit.

She doesn't say anything, so I start to pull away when her other hand grabs my hair, fisting it tightly and pulling my face back to her centre.

"Don't you fucking dare move, boss man. You promised to clean me up," she growls, and my dick jerks in my slacks.

I lift my eyes to hers and see an unhinged desire I know all too well. It's the same feeling she brings out in me.

Without another word, I smirk, leaning in and flattening my tongue against her clit. I can feel it throbbing against me as I slowly lap at her. I keep my eyes on hers and watch as she sucks in a sharp breath as her hips try to grind against my face.

"You want to control this, prairie?" I ask, using my teeth to nibble on her clit just enough to have her squirming in my hold.

"Please, just make me cum," she cries out, throwing her head back when I flick the tip of my tongue against her nub.

"I can do that. I'll feast on this pussy until you're so spent you can't think straight. Is that what you want?"

"Fuck. Christ, yes!"

"Anything for you, but that means I control how I fuck that smart mouth of yours when I'm done," I tell her, making her eyes drop back down to me.

I watch her lick her lips and feel the pre-cum begin to leak, begging for me to fuck her face now and not wait. I've waited this long. What's a few more minutes?

For the first time since meeting Shelby, I see her give in without a fight. More than that, I see just how badly she wants everything I've just promised her, and that look is my undoing.

# 22

## SHELBY

I KNOW I shouldn't give in so easily, but I'm reeling with the need to cum. All the emotions I've been dealing with recently have come to a head after my conversation with Jonathan, and the only person that can help me relieve the pressure is sitting between my legs. He's teasing me like it's his sworn mission to drive me insane, and he's winning.

He must see that in my eyes because, one second I'm looking at his eyes, and the next, he's going to town on me, teasing my clit and fucking me with his tongue.

"Oh, yes!" I scream out, bucking my hips against him the best I can with his grip on me.

When I feel his tongue part my folds as he drags

it down to my entrance, I tighten my hold on his hair and throw my head back.

"God, you taste so good," he mumbles against my core, sending waves of pleasure through me.

"Don't stop," I whisper, continuing to try and move my hips from his grip. "Let me go."

He huffs out a breath of annoyance before releasing me, allowing me to finally move my hips. I shouldn't taunt him; I know I shouldn't, but it's too good of an opportunity to pass up.

"Good boy," I tease.

His eyes fly up to mine with a fire burning inside of them, letting me know I'm in trouble now. Without a word, he brings his hand to my pussy and thrusts two fingers into me, fucking me hard and fast.

"You poked the bear, prairie. Now you're in for it," he growls out just before his tongue attacks my clit, forcing the hand holding me open to fall away.

"Yes. Fuck, yes!" I grind against his face, using his tongue and fingers to bring myself closer to climax while pulling hard at his hair with both hands.

He knows I'm close and doubles down his efforts, growling against my clit, making it vibrate as he adds a third finger.

Pleasure builds in my belly as he fucks me harder,

flicking his tongue against my clit in fast and hard motions and curling his fingers upward to hit that sweet spot inside of me with every thrust of his hand.

"Fuck, fuck," I chant as my orgasm slams into me from his skilled hands and mouth.

"Say it," he snarls, not letting up as the waves of pleasure course through me.

"No," I protest, knowing he can send me into a second orgasm if he keeps going, and he doesn't disappoint.

This time when I cum, I scream his name.

"Devlin! Yes! Fuck me, fuck me," I cry out, my entire body shattering at the pleasure he's drawn from my body.

"That's my filthy girl. Cumming for me so well," he praises me as he gently eases his fingers from my pussy.

"So good," I admit, making him smile.

"I told you I'd make you come alive, prairie. All you had to do was say my name."

He's such a cocky prick, but I love it.

Sitting up and pulling my legs from his shoulders, I lower them to the floor and stand up, ignoring the slight wobble in them.

"You promised me things, boss man. It's your

turn."

He stands with me and pulls me into him and cupping my cheek in his hand.

"Starving for my cock, hmm?" he teases before lowering his mouth to mine and kissing me.

I give in without thought, moving into him and allowing his tongue entrance as I wrap my arms around his neck to keep him close.

No man has ever been able to bring me to orgasm so easily, and as much as I hate to admit it, I know that at least a part of the reason is because of my feelings for him.

When his tongue touches mine, I taste myself on him, and it's a heady feeling. There's just something so hot about a man who can eat you out and then share your taste with you.

"Now," I say, biting his lip as I pull back, my hands going to the belt of his slacks.

"I'm in control, prairie," he says sternly, backing away from my touch. "On your knees."

There's a dominant tone to his voice that leaves no room for questioning, setting my soul on fire as I drop to my knees in front of him.

## DEVLIN

She's a vision as she kneels before me like my good prairie girl.

I didn't want to stop making her cum and tasting her release. Everything about her is addictive as hell, but the pain in my dick is getting worse with every passing moment. I need to feel her hot mouth wrapped around me while she chokes on my cock.

"A few orgasms and my prairie is compliant. Good to know." I step toward her, undoing my belt and the button on my pants before reaching into my boxers and stroking myself. "Yesss." It feels so goddamn good to finally give it some attention.

Shelby watches me with rapt attention as I pull myself from the confines of my boxers, whimpering when I start stroking my cock as I move within her reach.

"Open your mouth, prairie," I order, damn near cumming when she does just as she's told, sticking her tongue out for good measure.

"It's going to be hard, it's going to be fast, and it's going to be intense. Do you have a safe word?" I question, continuing to stroke myself as I watch her reaction.

"Red works just fine, but I won't be able to speak, right?" she asks, and I nod.

"Correct. I just wanted to make sure you had one." I move my cock to her mouth and drag the tip along her upper lip, painting it with pre-cum. "Tap my thigh three times if you need me to stop. Good?"

She nods and licks her lips, moaning when she tastes my cum, and I've had enough.

Once she opens her mouth again, I release my cock and grab her hair, shoving my cock deep into her throat. When she gags from the sheer force, I groan, pulling my hips back a little before thrusting them in again.

"God, yes." I pull almost all the way out to let her breathe as I look down into her watery eyes. "So good."

Her eyes flash with pleasure from the praise, and I slam my hips deeper once again, fucking her throat with a hard thrust.

"Hold on," I warn her before both of my hands grip her head. The moment she grips my thighs, I start fucking her throat, chasing a promised release as she chokes me down.

"Yes, shit. Take it, prairie," I grunt, fucking her harder and deeper, the heat of her throat a momentary nirvana.

When I feel my release build at the base of my spine, I give two more thrusts before pulling out and jerking my cock with cruelty.

"Hold out your tongue," I order, and the moment she does, I cum all over her face with a force that almost knocks me to the floor. "Dammit. Shit. Holy shit. Fuck."

When the final spurts of cum leave me, I watch Shelby lick her lips before wiping the cum off her face and licking it from her fingers with a groan.

"So good," she murmurs around her fingers when the last of it's been wiped from her face.

"Damn," I groan out, shaking my head like she's a dream. "That was the hottest shit I've ever seen."

She smirks at me, going to stand, but I clamp my hand down on her shoulder.

"You missed some."

"What?" she asks, looking confused, and I smirk.

"You missed some. Clean it up, prairie." I nod down to my shoe, and her eyes flare.

I can see she wants to fight me, but there's another part of her that's curious, so I lift my eyebrow, silently waiting for her to make a choice.

"There's my good little whore," I praise, stroking the top of her head when she bends down to lick the drops of cum off of my dress shoe. "So fucking perfect."

# 23

# DEVLIN

By the time Lo and I get cleaned up and changed, it's nearing three in the morning, and we're both fucking beat.

Once I set the alarm and lock up the club, I walk her to her car, not liking the idea of her driving when she's this tired.

"Let me drive you home," I say, knowing better than to try and force it on her. It's not like she doesn't make this drive every night after work.

She smirks. "I'm fine, and I need the car. I'm opening the shop at noon for Liv."

Well, at least she'll still get some sleep.

"Let me know when you're home safe," I tell her, pulling her into my chest for a hug.

"Yeah, okay, stalker man. You'll probably know

I'm home before I even get the door unlocked," she smarts off, earning a sharp slap on the ass.

"That mouth of yours is going to get you into a lot of trouble, Lo. Watch it."

Even through the exhaustion, she cracks a smile, and it warms me inside.

"You like my mouth, boss man. Don't try and lie now."

Brat. Fuck, she's amazing.

"Get your smartass self into that car and drive home." I lean down, nipping her nose with my teeth, and she giggles.

"Sir, yes, sir!" She salutes me before opening the door and sitting in the front seat. "You're going to be watching me all night anyway. Why don't you just come sleep on the couch?"

"Ouch," I gasp, clutching my chest like I'm wounded. "I give you the best orgasms of your life, and you still demote me to couch duty. That hurts, prairie. That hurts."

She shakes her head, rolling her eyes. "Shut up and meet me there."

I close her door, watching her drive away as I get into my vehicle, quickly catching up to her and following her home.

* * *

"You've got to be kidding me," I grumble to myself when Lo walks into the living room after we've had a few hours of sleep.

"What was that?" she asks in such a sweet voice that I know she heard exactly what I said.

"You're washing dogs... in that?"

Look. I'm not the type of man to tell a woman what is and is not appropriate to wear, but five-inch heels just seems like it's a bit much.

"Ha! No, it's just inventory and appointment bookings today." She looks down at the heels she's paired with black jeans and a pink top. "I have sneakers at the shop, anyway. I just forgot to bring them home last time I was working, and I have a shift tonight." She shrugs, moving to the couch and straddling my lap.

"Lo," I warn her, knowing we don't have time to start anything right now. She has to be at the shop in half an hour.

"Dev," she mocks.

I move my hands to her ass, gripping it tightly.

"Don't start something you can't finish, prairie girl," I growl, pushing her core against my growing length.

"There is such a thing as a quickie, you know," she teases.

Moving fast, I lift her off me and lay her down on the table beneath me. "The first time I'm deep inside you is going to be anything but quick, prairie."

She whimpers and it's a sound I usually love, but something is off about it. Lowering my weight to take her face in my hands, I search her eyes.

"What's wrong, Lo? Shelby? Talk to me," I beg.

"I,I—" she stammers, slamming her eyes shut like she's in pain. "Off. Please," she whispers, her entire body vibrating.

Her words haven't even registered before I'm standing and pulling her into my arms, sitting back on the couch and cradling her to my chest to comfort her.

I don't know what the hell is happening, but something upset her, and I will figure out what so I can avoid ever doing it again.

"Hey, hey now. What happened?" I rock her against me as her body shakes, and her breath comes out in shallow, sharp pants.

"Can—can't...hard surface. Too much," she says in short sentences, trying to organize her thoughts.

"You can't have your back against a hard

surface?" I ask, hating myself for just assuming she would be up for anything.

"Triggered. Last night…remembered too much… need time." She shakes her head to clear it.

I try to read between the lines to understand what she's trying to tell me.

"Something about my lying over you triggered something. Am I understanding that right?" I ask her gently, torn between the need to calm her and getting to the bottom of what triggered her.

She takes a deep, shuddering breath before forcing herself to sit up and look at me. Her eyes are lined with unshed tears, making me want to hunt down her worst nightmares and destroy them so she never has to feel this way again.

"I'm usually okay," she whispers quietly, her voice shaking a bit. "Just… Jonathan knew something last night that I never wanted another living soul to know, and it—" She pauses, looking to the side and glancing outside. "I guess the idea of someone else knowing just freaks me out. It brought up a lot of memories. Though," she says, moving her head back to look at me.

"What?" I run my hands up and down her back to try and soothe her. I have a feeling I'm not going to like what she's about to tell me.

She takes another deep breath, this one stronger than before as she works to get her walls back up. She's not blocking me out this time, but clearly this runs deep for her.

"No one has touched me since that night on the floor," she says, watching for my reaction.

My body stiffens as my mind flashes back to the only night she could possibly be referring to.

"Breton," I growl his name, and she scrunches her nose in disgust.

"Don't use his last name. My best friend bears the same name, and she doesn't deserve to ever be grouped into the same arena as him. As them," she sneers.

She's referring to Ben and their father. I still cannot understand why anyone would want to hurt someone as sweet as my best friend's woman, but Ben and his father aren't normal. Like Jon said, they're sociopaths. They feel nothing.

"You're right." I nod, agreeing with her. "You said you knew him that night. Afterward, I assumed it was just because he was Olivia's brother. That's not it, though. Is it, Lo?"

I hear the darkness in my own voice as the realization of what that asshole has probably done to her floods my mind.

"No. It's not," she admits, looking ashamed.

"Shelby, look at me," I tell her, grabbing her chin and turning her face to make sure she's paying attention to what I'm about to say. "Whatever that bastard did to you, it was not your fault."

She sniffles, those tears finally slipping past her beautiful eyes to run down her cheeks.

"I was sixteen," she says so softly I almost miss it.

"I should bring him back to life and beat him to death myself," I growl, tightening my hold on her.

"I hear he suffered a great deal," she says, a small smile on her face as she continues to cry. She leans forward to rest her forehead on mine. "He's gone."

"He's still haunting you," I remind her, and she swallows hard.

"It's just really raw in my mind right now. I'll be okay soon."

I let go of her chin, moving my head back to kiss her forehead.

"So, your back on a hard surface with me towering over you? That's what triggered you?" I ask her, stroking her hair gently, and she nods.

"Yes, but again, I think it's because this is all so fresh. And Tiffany," she says before stopping.

Narrowing my eyes on her, she shakes her head.

"I don't know anything for sure, and I don't think she would ever say anything if things did happen."

She's probably right. Tiffany is one of my girls that I worry the most about. She lives in an extremely rough neighbourhood, is a single mom, and she takes care of her ailing mother and grand-mother alone too. Money is tight for her.

It doesn't matter how much I pay her or how many hours she works; it's not enough. I know she gets money on the side, and there is absolutely nothing I can do about it.

Legally, I know it's frowned upon to sleep with your customers, and seen as disrespectful to the owner, but I know she's safer with most of them than she would be turning tricks on the corner, so I let it slide. And only for her because I've seen how hard she struggle to survive. Her kids need her around, and I refuse to be the asshole that fires her because she will become another one of those statistics I despise so fucking much.

I know Ben hasn't treated her well. Any night she has left with him or another customer, I've always had one of the guards following her at a distance to make sure she gets away safely and back to her kids. They all tell me the same thing. She doesn't fight him. She cries a lot when he leaves, but she doesn't stop it, and she keeps going back.

We can't help her more than making sure she's safe, but now that he's dead, she should be fine. He was the only customer that ever hurt her, and I will continue to watch out for my employees because it's who I am.

"Can you do me a favour while you're at the shop?" I ask her, and she tilts her head to the side with a frown between her brows.

"What?"

"Think of anything that might trigger you and make a list. I don't want to set you off again."

"Yeah. Sure, boss man. I can do that."

"Good girl. Thank you."

## SHELBY

"ARE YOU OKAY?" Liv asks me sweetly.

I smile at her, so fucking thankful for my best friend.

"I'm okay, I promise."

She surprised me with a video call directly after my dance tonight.

When I had walked out of the changing room, the girls working hooted when they took in the bruises on my ass that Devlin had made last night. I still can't believe we did that shit at work. He may own the place, but it still feels wrong in a forbidden sort of way.

I'm a stripper sleeping with my much older boss. God, I'm such a cliche.

"Out of curiosity, how long does it take to get

that makeup off at the end of the night?" Liv asks with a giggle that warms my heart.

That genuine sweetness is just one of the things I love so much about my best friend.

"With that makeup melting milk shit you bought me for Christmas, it actually isn't too bad. Although, when it's one in the morning it can feel like hours," I whine with a smile on my face.

"I don't know how you do it, Shelbs," she says, shaking her head. "You always look stunning when you wear makeup. Whenever I attempt it, I end up looking like a baby penguin did my makeup while flying through the air high on sugar."

I laugh so hard I start to choke as Jonathan pipes up in the background.

"You don't need makeup. You are absolutely stunning and perfect just as you are, sunflower."

I watch her swoon at his words, and I hate to admit that I was wrong about him. Actually, no, I was right about him being a murderer. I was just wrong about him being bad for my bestie. It seems he's what she's needed all along. He complements her in a way that just makes her light shine brighter.

"Penguins don't fly, Liv," I point out when I've finished laughing, and she smiles.

"Exactly. That shows you just how bad it really

is." She winks at me before telling me to have a good night and hanging up the phone to join her man for a movie night.

I bet she's suckered him into some sappy movie, too. He's so fucked for her that she could ask him to watch *Barney,* and he'd happily agree to it.

"Cherry!" Paul hollers from the door.

"Yeah?"

"Beth needs your help on the floor. You good?"

"Yeah, be out in a sec!"

* * *

"You rang, your Highness?" I snark at Beth when I get to the bar, and she throws a towel at me.

"Shut that pretty face of yours, brat, and help me with table fifteen. They've been sitting there for ten minutes, and no one has been able to get to them yet."

I wince, knowing that won't make them very happy. No one likes to wait for that long before at least having their drink order taken.

"On it!"

Taking a deep breath, I pull the chest of my shirt town a bit to offer more cleavage than I normally would, aiming to soften the blow of having to wait.

"Hey, gentleman, my name is Cherry, and I'll be your server tonight!"

Their eyes land on me with interest, sneers disappearing from their faces when they see the top of my tits sticking out.

"Why, hey there, Cherry. How are you doing tonight?" one of them drawls, slurring like he's already been drinking.

I make a mental note to mention that to Beth while smiling at him.

"I am great!" I look between them. "Sorry for the longer than usual wait. We're busier than normal at the moment."

"That's alright. Not being served until now just means we got luckiest by getting the prettiest girl here," another says, laying it on thick.

Ugh, why do they have to be so predictable? It's not like I want to be swept off my feet, but couldn't they at least find it inside themselves to be a bit more original from time to time?

"Lucky me," I purr, laying it on thick. "What will it be tonight, boys?" I ask, ready to get out of here.

"When are you going to dance tonight?" the first one asks.

"I already did. You just missed me." I snap my fingers in a darn motion.

"I guess we'll just have to make do then," the one next to me says before his hand grabs my ass.

I stiffen, hoping to fuck boss man isn't around right now because he will lose his shit. Not only because there's a no touching rule for the floor, but because he's threatened to murder anyone that dares to touch me.

Really, he's going to need to chill a bit on that one given my job. There's no way I'm quitting, either, and he knows it.

"Ah ah, no touching." I back away with a giggle, trying to play it off, but the drunk one scoffs.

"You're paid to be a slut."

Now that pisses me off.

"Listen here yo—"

"I'm sorry, but I'm going to have to ask you to leave," Devlin growls behind me, and I know this is going to go to shit.

"Who the hell are you to tell us what to do?" the drunk idiot challenges him, but instead of getting angry, Devlin moves in front of me and leans over the table to get in the man's face.

"I own this place. But more than that, I'm friends with Jonathan Carmichael." Every man's face at the table drains of colour, and Devlin smirks. "You know, your boss?"

The guy that originally grabbed me clears his throat. "Hey, we aren't causing trouble," he says, trying to barter his way out of this.

Of course, he's a lawyer. Probably not a very good one, but at least he's smart enough to be fearful of Jonathan.

"You touched one of my girls," Dev says, standing up and rolling the sleeves of his dress shirt to his elbows.

Fuck, that is so hot.

"We're sorry," he apologizes, and Devlin shrugs. Ever the boss in control of a situation, he waves over Paul and another one of the guards.

"I appreciate that, but the rules were clear when you entered, and you broke them. Now, I need you to leave."

They look ready to argue until more guards show up. Realizing they don't stand a chance, they follow the guards toward the door, and I breathe a sigh of relief.

Until he turns to look at me, his eyes filled with danger and promise.

"Office, Ms. Engels. Now."

Oh, yeah. I'm about to get fucked and hard. Yum.

# DEVLIN

I FUCKING TOLD HER, and now her ass is going to pay for that prick touching her.

As soon as the door to my office is locked behind us, I grab her hips and turn her around, placing her palms on my desk.

"This okay?" I check in with her.

"Fuck yes," she groans, and I smile. My dick is so fucking hard for her right now, just knowing I'm about to mark her perfect skin.

"Good. If you think it's getting too much, call out the word yellow. I don't want to trigger you again," I tell her as I rip the thong from her body.

"As long as I'm not pressed against the desk in any way, I'm good, boss," she promises, and fucking hell, I am here for it.

"Stay perfectly still while I redden this ass of yours," I order, palming the globes of her ass.

"God, you're intense."

I smirk. "You've barely scratched the surface, prairie."

It's the last thing I say before raising my palm in the air and bringing it down hard on her ass. The sound echoes through the room, mixing with her sharp intake of breath and setting me that much more on edge.

Slap after slap, cheek after cheek, I go hard until she's a whimpering wet mess, barely able to stand. Her ass is a bright red that matches the anger inside of me from that asshole daring to touch what's mine.

Moving my fingers to her centre, I groan when I realize how truly soaked she is. "Someone enjoyed that a little too much," I taunt, rolling my finger over her clit, making her cry out.

"Shit!"

"If you cum without my cock inside of you, prairie, you're going to regret it," I warn her, moving the fingers to her entrance and sliding a lone one inside her channel while my other works to pull my aching cock free.

"Then hurry the fuck up and stop teasing me," she whines, grinding into my hand.

Once my cock is free, I slap her ass once more and pull my fingers from her core and move them to her mouth. "Suck."

She opens her mouth and takes me in, moaning as she sucks her juices from my fingers, reminding me of just how skilled she is with that mouth of hers.

Next time, I'll give her more control and see what she really can do with it.

I move in behind her as she continues to suck on my fingers. Grasping my cock, I line it up with her entrance before thrusting in deep without warning. Her screams of shock and pleasure are muffled around my fingers, and I laugh darkly when I'm buried to the hilt.

Pulling my fingers from her mouth, I move them to her throat and gently squeeze. "Mine."

She moans and wiggles her ass against me, silently begging me to fuck her.

"Please," she whimpers, and I laugh again, getting a thrill out of how desperately she wants me to claim her.

"You beg so nicely," I hiss into her ear, pulling my hips back before slamming my cock back inside of her tight heat, groaning when her warmth envelopes me again.

"You want me to beg for this cock?" she taunts, wiggling her ass and deliberately squeezing around me.

"Yeah, prairie, I do," I groan.

"Fuck me, boss man. Fuck me so hard and dirty I feel you for days. Make me yours."

"As you wish."

I pull away and start pounding into her, my hand moving into her hair to fist it tightly as her sweet cunt sucks me deep with every forward movement.

"No one touches you," I grind out, fucking her even harder as her screams of pleasure drive me to dizzying heights.

"I know," she rasps, pushing her hips back to meet my rhythm, fucking me back with all the energy she has while bracing her hands on the desk.

I'll never be able to work in this office again.

"Mine. If it hadn't been at the club, I would have slit that bastard's throat for daring to lay a hand on you." God, she feels so fucking good. I'm already close to cumming but not ready for it to be over yet.

"Please!" she cries and begs, her voice rising with every scream as I rut into her cunt.

"I'm going to mark you inside just like I did the

outside, so you never forget who possesses you," I warn her, and she freezes.

"Condom."

I laugh and fuck her faster, yanking on her hair and forcing her to stand with her back against me.

"You have the implant, Shelby, and I'm clean. Unless you're really against it, I'm going to cum deep in this cunt from now until forever."

She grunts, throwing her head back onto my shoulder while I move my free hand to her tit and squeeze roughly.

"You're a fucking caveman," she says, and I lick her beck before moving my hand up to grab her chin and turn her head toward me. "Answer me."

I feel her pussy fluttering around me and know she's about to cum, but I want a goddamn answer first.

"No cumming without me. That means I need an answer, prairie," I hiss, trying to hold off my own release as I feel the tingles in my spine and my balls getting heavy.

"Yes. Fuck, yes. Cum in me and do whatever the fuck you want. Just let me cum!" she screams and bears down on me, flying over the edge when my mouth lands on hers.

Her release sets off my own, making me roar into

her mouth as jet after jet leaves me, filling her up so full she can never doubt it's me she damn well belongs to.

When we've both caught out breaths, I start to slowly move inside of her again, our joined releases making it easy to slide in and out. I'm too hard for this to end here.

Something tells me this will go on all night. Eventually, we'll have to head back to one of our places, but right now, I'm not ready to leave her warmth.

"Good girl," I praise her, nudging her nose with mine. "You're mine forever, Shelby. We already knew it, but tonight sealed your fate."

"Meaning?" she asks with a smirk.

"Meaning, I am so irrevocably obsessed and in love with you, you'll never get rid of me."

Her pussy squeezes around me as her smile widens.

"Good, because I feel the same way, boss man. There's nowhere you can go that I won't follow."

I pull away, looking down into her eyes.

"Say it." She knows what I want, and she'll give it to me.

"I love you, boss man. Now make love to me so we can go home and do this all over again."

Fuck. Yes.

## THE END

For up to date news on the Dark Series and more, make sure you join my **NEWSLETTER TODAY!** (www.cassiehargrove.com/links)

# COMING UP NEXT...

Thank you so much for reading Shelby and Devlin's Novella! I really hope you liked it at least half as much as you did Jonathan and Olivia's story because I loved writing every part of it.

So, now that you've read Dark Longing, you may be wondering what's next.

If you've grabbed the FREE BONUS CHAPTER for Dark Torment, then you've already met the next character.

**BOOK 3 OF THE DARK SERIES WILL BE JONATHAN AND OLIVIA'S SON ANDREW, AND WILL RELEASE LATER ON THIS YEAR.**

(Most of my upcoming releases don't currently have release dates right now because I'm working through some health issues that need me to not be stressing out over deadlines...but they're still being worked on!)

# ABOUT CASSIE HARGROVE

Cassie Hargrove is an author of all things romance. She is a stay at home mom of three crazy kids. Seven year old autistic twins, and a sassy four year old that 100% takes after her mother.

She lives in a small town with her husband and children, three cats and a dog. Writing is something she's enjoyed her entire life. It brings an element of calm into the chaos of life.

Newsletter

## The Revenge Diaries

(A Series of Dark/Very Dark Standalones)

1: Trick or Revenge

2: Beautiful Revenge (Original and Less Triggering Versions)

3: Love's Dark Revenge (Coming Soon)

## Standalones

Depravity: An Extremely Taboo Novel (Co-Write with Seven Rue)

The Art of Freedom and Growth (A Depravity Extended Epilogue) (Co-Write with Seven Rue)

## The Deadly Seven

A Co-Write with Story Brooks

1: Obsession

2: Seduction

3: Devotion

4: Salvation

5: Justified Retribution: Kristen's Story (Coming March 6)

## Dark Series

1: Dark Torment

2: Dark Longing

## Erotic Shorts

Taken By Him

Intern-al Affairs

Bound To Him

Santa Daddy's Naughty Baby

CASSIE HARGROVE WRITING AS A.L. RYAN

Roommates: A Dark Sapphic Romance

## Forbidden Kinks

Book 0.5:

Still His

Previously Published as Still by Cassie Hargrove

Made in United States
Orlando, FL
24 August 2024

50716146R10124